Understanding

Beowulf

New and future titles in the Understanding Great Literature series include:

Understanding

Beowulf

UNDERSTANDING GREAT LITERATURE

Tom Streissguth

LUCENT
BOOKS®

THOMSON
★
™
GALE

829.3
STR

San Diego • Detroit • New York • San Francisco • Cleveland
New Haven, Conn. • Waterville, Maine • London • Munich

LIBRARY OF CONGRESS CATALOGING-IN-PUBLICATION DATA

Streissguth, Thomas, 1958–
    Understanding Beowulf / by Thomas Streissguth
p. cm. — (Understanding great literature)
Summary: Discusses the authorship, character analysis, historical background, plot and themes of Beowulf.
Includes bibliographical references and index.
    ISBN 1-56006-861-2 (alk. paper)
    1. Beowulf—Juvenile literature. 2. Epic poetry, English (Old)—History and criticism—Juvenile literature. 3. Scandinavia—In literature—Juvenile literature. 4. Monsters in literature—Juvenile literature. 5. Dragons in literature—Juvenile literature. 6. Heroes in literature—Juvenile literature. [1. Beowulf. 2. Epic poetry.] I. Title. II. Series
    PR1585.S77 2004
    829'.3—dc21

                               2002156114

Printed in the United States of America

Contents

FOREWORD

"Except for a living man, there is nothing more wonderful than a book!" wrote the widely respected nineteenth-century teacher and writer Charles Kingsley. A book, he continued, "is a message to us from human souls we never saw. And yet these [books] arouse us, terrify us, teach us, comfort us, open our hearts to us as brothers." There are many different kinds of books, of course; and Kingsley was referring mainly to those containing literature—novels, plays, short stories, poems, and so on. In particular, he had in mind those works of literature that were and remain widely popular with readers of all ages and from many walks of life.

Such popularity might be based on one or several factors. On the one hand, a book might be read and studied by people in generation after generation because it is a literary classic, with characters and themes of universal relevance and appeal. Homer's epic poems, the *Iliad* and the *Odyssey*, Chaucer's *Canterbury Tales*, Shakespeare's *Hamlet* and *Romeo and Juliet*, and Dickens's *A Christmas Carol* fall into this category. Some popular books, on the other hand, are more controversial. Mark Twain's *Huckleberry Finn* and J.D. Salinger's *The Catcher in the Rye*, for instance, have their legions of devoted fans who see them as great literature; while others view them as less than worthy because of their racial depictions, profanity, or other factors.

Still another category of popular literature includes realistic modern fiction, including novels such as Robert Cormier's *I Am the Cheese* and S.E. Hinton's *The Outsiders*. Their keen social insights and sharp character portrayals have consistently reached out to and captured the imaginations of many teenagers and young adults; and for this reason they are often assigned and studied in schools.

These and other similar works have become the "old standards" of the literary scene. They are the ones that people most often read, discuss, and study; and each has, by virtue of its content, critical success, or just plain longevity, earned the right to be the subject of a book examining its content. (Some, of course, like the *Iliad* and *Hamlet*, have been the subjects of numerous books already; but their literary stature is so lofty that there can never be too many books about them!) For millions of readers and students in one generation after another, each of these works becomes, in a sense, an adventure in appreciation, enjoyment, and learning.

The main purpose of Lucent's Understanding Great Literature series is to aid the reader in that ongoing literary adventure. Each volume in the series focuses on a single literary work that a majority of critics and teachers view as a classic and/or that is widely studied and discussed in schools. A typical volume first tells why the work in question is important. Then follow detailed overviews of the author's life, the work's historical background, its plot, its characters, and its themes. Numerous quotes from the work, as well as by critics and other experts, are interspersed throughout and carefully documented with footnotes for those who wish to pursue further research. Also included is a list of ideas for essays and other student projects relating to the work, an appendix of literary criticisms and analyses by noted scholars, and a comprehensive annotated bibliography.

The great nineteenth-century American poet Henry David Thoreau once quipped: "Read the best books first, or you may not have a chance to read them at all." For those who are reading or about to read the "best books" in the literary canon, the comprehensive, thorough, and thoughtful volumes of the Understanding Great Literature series are indispensable guides and sources of enrichment.

The Strange and Eloquent Music of *Beowulf*

The poem *Beowulf*, written by an anonymous poet at an uncertain time and in a nearly incomprehensible ancient language, has haunted literature students of the English-speaking world for several generations. Within this work of over three thousand lines, a hero named Beowulf battles supernatural monsters, knights boast of courageous deeds within torchlit drinking halls, and kings offer gilded swords and armor as rewards for victory in hand-to-hand combat. Blood feuds last for generations, and tribes of violent pagans clash over treasure and territory. The heroes stand as if giants, and the society is tribal and strange. An atmosphere of fear, dread, and doom surrounds the action—and there is no happy ending. There seems little indeed to connect the events recounted in *Beowulf* with the concerns of a twenty-first-century reader or the contemporary world.

Still, *Beowulf* rewards those patient enough to plumb its depths. The poem is a witness to the past and to the thoughts and fears of people living at the dawn of medieval civilization. Entering the world of *Beowulf* is a way of understanding this past in a way that cannot be duplicated by studying the remains of crumbling monuments and churches. Through the dimly lit hall and the dark and haunted forests imagined by the poet, a reader can experience a world of heroes and kings. The reader can return to Anglo-Saxon England, where poets and audiences alike feared the supernatural and believed in superhuman deeds.

A painting depicts a medieval battle. Legendary battles from the early Middle Ages provided the author of Beowulf *with inspiration for the epic tale.*

The Work of Reading *Beowulf*

A first reading of *Beowulf* will confuse and frustrate any ordinary reader. The story stops and starts, takes unexpected turns, and changes its tone and meaning with little apparent reason and absolutely no rhyming. The structure of the poem seems haphazard, as if a group of stories were simply drawn out of a helmet and placed end to end with no overriding plan. Characters and places are given various names, which are difficult for the modern English speaker to pronounce or remember. Long passages of genealogy, in which lists of ancestors and relatives appear, bring the action to a grinding halt. The poet veers off track by describing, praising, and condemning unrelated events and people.

These problems arise from the fact that *Beowulf* comes from an oral tradition in which stories were sung to an audience, not silently read by an individual. An oral epic like *Beowulf* demands different storytelling skills than does written poetry. To entertain a listening audience, the poet must create frequent changes of scene and mood. This means skipping over some events and repeating others, veering into digressions meant to illuminate and contrast the action of the main story, and simply improvising on favored themes and characters.

A second problem for the contemporary reader is foreknowledge—the revelation of future events and the outcome of the story. There were few secrets for the original audience of *Beowulf*. From similar stories retold hundreds of times, the members of this audience knew the hero, knew the kings and queens and knights he encounters, knew the dragons and monsters, and knew the ending. For the Anglo-Saxon listener, a performance of *Beowulf* was like a performance of familiar music, which was judged not on the plot or the finale but on the skill in the telling.

In the lines of *Beowulf*, the modern reader must try to understand a way of life that disappeared more than a millennium ago. The characters of *Beowulf* live among small bands of warriors, who owe personal loyalty to a chieftain, who take personal vengeance for wrongs committed against them, and who carry on blood feuds lasting for generations. These characters look on independence and solitude—virtues much celebrated by many modern poets—as things to be greatly feared and avoided.

The reader will also sense a conflict between two worlds— the old world of the pagans and the new world of the Christians. Although the poet reveals himself as a devout Christian, the characters of his story live in a transitional world in which the pagan ways are slowly but surely surrendering to Christian virtues. The shifting worldview gives the poem a sense of inner conflict, mirroring in some ways the violent combats that take place within the story. The *Beowulf* reader is never quite certain which ethos—pagan or Christian—will, or should, triumph.

The Survival of *Beowulf*

Beowulf has posed problems for historians that match the difficulties faced by ordinary readers. Many mysteries surround the composition of *Beowulf* and the identity of its author. The first copy of *Beowulf* appeared in a manuscript that dates to about 1000 A.D. The poem was recorded by scribes who collected it with several other works in a bound book known as a codex. The codex made its way into the collection of Lawrence Nowell and then into the library of the Englishman Robert Cotton, a collector of antique books who lived during the time of Queen Elizabeth I (the late sixteenth century). Cotton gathered his library of old books in a series of bookcases, and on top of each case was the bust of a Roman emperor or a famous figure of ancient history. The bookcase that contained the *Beowulf* codex had a bust of the emperor Vitellus, and from this fact the book was catalogued as "Cotton Vitellus A xv," or the fifteenth book in row A of the Vitellus bookcase.

The old lettering of the codex, damaged in a fire in 1731, was transcribed by an Icelandic scholar, Grimur Jonsson Thorkelin, in 1787. After Thorkelin made his transcription, translators in England and the United States set to the very difficult task of rendering the old language into modern English. For years, translating *Beowulf* was a standard assignment of university literature courses, in which students labored with dusty dictionaries to guess at the words, meaning, and flow of the original work. Only those who have studied for many years can read the poem in the original, and even in translation the poem attracts only a small general audience. For many contemporary readers, *Beowulf* seems a literary relic, a strange and difficult work that belongs to a distant, unfamiliar world.

Seamus Heaney, who finished the most recent and one of the most popular translations of *Beowulf*, points out that those who look on *Beowulf* as a dusty relic are missing out: "What we are dealing with is a work of the greatest imaginative vitality, a masterpiece where the structuring of the tale is as elaborate as the beautiful contrivances of its language. Its narrative elements may belong to a previous age but as a work of art it lives in its own continuous present, equal to our knowledge of reality in the present time."[1]

Why translate and study this strange, ancient, and difficult work? First, as a historical document, it teaches much about a little-known period of medieval history. *Beowulf* was the first major poem in English literature and offers a close look at the everyday life during this mysterious age. Many critics also look on the poem as an important foundation of English literature, a touchstone from which all later poetry and literature in the English language developed. Finally, within the complex narrative the reader will find an exciting and suspenseful story, a tale recounted by a skilled and eloquent literary artist. *Beowulf* has been much studied, but it is also a poem to be enjoyed.

The editors of *Classical and Medieval Literature Criticism* describe the virtues of *Beowulf* as follows:

> This anonymous work is many things at once: artifact, history, epic, elegy, folklore, and linguistic document, to name a few. The poem is remarkable both as a historical milestone and as a work of literature.... *Beowulf* is an essential object of study for linguists, historians, and literary critics alike, for whom the poem is a window on medieval culture, an Old English document of the first order, and a deeply felt study of man's fate in an uncertain world.[2]

In *Beowulf,* therefore, readers are studying much more than an old poem. They are witnessing the origins of their culture and language and the foundation of the centuries of English literature to come.

CHAPTER ONE

A Mysterious Author, a Mysterious Time

An epic poem 3,182 lines in length, *Beowulf* describes a vanished world of kings, heroes, monsters, treasure, heroic combat, and supernatural events. The date of the poem is uncertain, but most experts believe it was originally written in the eighth century. This was the time of Anglo-Saxon Britain, a land of petty kings and warlords who fought constantly along ever-changing frontiers. For historians, this period of time remains elusive and largely unknown. Few buildings survive from the Anglo-Saxon period, and there is little evidence of how people really lived. Important events have become legends. For instance, the war between the native "Britons" and the invading Anglo-Saxons, who came from the continent of Europe, gave rise to the story of King Arthur.

Beowulf is another legend from the time of the Anglo-Saxons. Nobody knows who created *Beowulf*. The only manuscript copy of the poem was created by two scribes centuries after the poem was first composed. The copyists did not name the author, nor did they date the work or identify themselves. To draw conclusions on the identity and the time of the *Beowulf* poet, historians have only the evidence of the poem itself.

The First *Beowulf* Book

Beowulf exists in the form of a single hand-copied manuscript. Historians of the poem believe that this manuscript dates to around 1000 A.D. and that the poem itself dates to the late seventh or early eighth centuries. These dates are uncertain, however, and the mystery of *Beowulf*'s true origins remains. Who copied *Beowulf*, and why did they undertake this work? Were the scribes working from memory, transcribing a recital of the poem, or copying an older manuscript that has since been lost?

The lines of *Beowulf* are recorded in what is known as the Nowell Codex, after the English collector Lawrence Nowell,

Tenth-Century Anglo-Saxon England

15

A page from the Beowulf *manuscript, dated to circa 1000 A.D. This manuscript
is the only surviving copy of the story and it is kept in the British Museum.*

the first-known owner of the work. In medieval times, codices (handwritten bound books) were rare and valuable: They were considered small, portable treasures, made for the purpose of keeping and preserving the worthy writings of an earlier time. Each book was unique, copied by hand on sheets of parchment or vellum, which were then folded into groups of pages known as quires. Rather than containing just a single work of prose or poetry, many books held large collections of works very different in style and purpose.

There are several different works within the codex that contains *Beowulf*. This book also contains *The Passion of St. Christopher*, a travel story known as the *Wonders of the East*, and a *Letter of Alexander the Great to Aristotle*. After *Beowulf* there is also a fragment of a poem known as *Judith*. (Historians have speculated that the scribes who set down the poem may have wanted to collect several works that exhibited natural or human wonders, such as the monsters and heroes of *Beowulf*.) By analyzing the handwriting, scholars have determined that one scribe recorded the first three works and the first 1,939 lines of *Beowulf*, and a different scribe recorded the rest of the poem as well as the work that follows, the *Book of Judith*.

Most historians believe that the *Beowulf* manuscript, as the work of two different scribes, must be a copy of an earlier work. According to this theory, sometime after the poem was originally created—perhaps centuries—it was set down on parchment by the two anonymous scribes. The original work, in whatever form it took, was then lost. But when was this original work created?

The Dating of *Beowulf*

Scholars have been debating the true date of *Beowulf* since 1815, when the Icelandic scholar Grimur Jonsson Thorkelin became the first to transcribe the poem from its original manuscript. Thorkelin believed that *Beowulf* was an old Danish poem that dated to the fourth or fifth centuries A.D. Other scholars were quick to disagree with Thorkelin. Nicolaus Outzen believed the poem to be much later, based on *Beowulf's* many references to the Christian religion and Christian morality. Because of its language, setting, and characters, *Beowulf* undoubtedly came from northern Europe, the land of the Anglo-Saxons. However, because northern Europe had not yet been converted to Christianity in the fifth century, and the poem contains Christian references, Outzen believed that the poem could not be from that time. Instead, it had to be written some time later, after the conversion of the pagan Anglo-Saxons to Christianity (which began during the late sixth century).

In 1817 the scholar N.F.S. Grundtvig showed that the character of Hygelac, an important king of *Beowulf*, was based on a historic figure, the Scandinavian raider Chlochilaichus. This raider was described in the history of the medieval scholar Gregory of Tours, who described an attack on the northern coast of Europe that resulted in Chlochilaichus's death. Since the raid took place between 515 and 530, *Beowulf* could not have been written before that time.

Since the time of these early critics, many scholars have used the evidence of language to date the poem. *Beowulf* was written in the West Saxon dialect of Old English, the language used by the Anglo-Saxon people of early medieval Britain. Old English is a member of the Germanic family of languages, and it shares certain grammar and some root vocabulary words with modern German. The West Saxon dialect was used in northern England before that region was conquered by Scandinavian raiders. (This conquest began with the Viking raid on the Lindisfarne monastery in 792 A.D., an event that preceded several decades of devastating raids on English coasts and towns.)

Many scholars agree with critic Dorothy Whitelock that praising Scandinavians had probably gone out of fashion after the Viking raids began:

The poem is surely pre-Viking Age. It may be true that we should not attach an exaggerated importance to the high terms of praise and respect with which the poet speaks of the Danes and their rulers.... Yet, I doubt whether he would have spoken in these terms during the Viking Age.... It is not how men like to hear the people described who are burning their homes, pillaging their churches, ravaging their cattle and crops, killing their countrymen or carrying them off into slavery.[3]

But a few critics disagree with Whitelock and see the manuscript copy of *Beowulf* as an original creation of the late tenth or early eleventh centuries. According to this theory, the scribes who recorded the poem either created it themselves or transcribed it from a new work in a different form. The scholar Kevin S. Kiernan believes *Beowulf* was created by two different poets and that their works were later combined. He also believes the poets were celebrating Danish history and that they worked during the time of Canute, the Danish Viking who ruled England during the early eleventh century:

It is not hard to imagine how Anglo-Saxon poems like *Beowulf* might have emerged during the reign of Knut [Canute] the Great as an aesthetic aftermath of the Danish Conquest.... There are remarkable affinities between the *Beowulf* poet and the Norse skalds [poets] and storytellers who thrived in the age of Knut.... The poet begins with a dedicatory salute to the founding of Knut's royal Scylding dynasty.[4]

Besides the original date of *Beowulf*, critics and historians have many other fields of debate over *Beowulf*. Two of the most interesting questions surrounding *Beowulf* have always been the poet's identity and the nature of his work. Who wrote *Beowulf*? Was he a public performer, a literary poet, or

A fleet of Viking ships departs on a 933 A.D. *raid of England. Beowulf takes place in Scandinavia (home of the Vikings) and some of its characters are identifiable figures of Scandinavian history.*

a monk? Did this poet intend his work as a sung performance or as a written work to be read from a book?

Beowulf as Performance Art

Most scholars believe that the original *Beowulf* story was a folktale, that it was known to entertainers known as scops, and that the *Beowulf* poet was one of these performers. The scops sung tales of old for the entertainment of kings and the members of their courts. The stories of these Anglo-Saxon poets, already familiar to their audiences, celebrated the deeds of long-dead kings and heroes who played an important role in the founding of the nation.

While they listened, the audiences carefully measured the skill of the performer in weaving a good story and in giving the work his own voice and style. The audience judged the scop by his ability to turn an everyday tale into an individual and artistically satisfying performance. In turn, the scop measured his audience when performing. Before a group of battle-weary knights, for example, the scop may have praised the deeds of fighting men. To earn greater appreciation and reward, the scop who sang for a king may have complimented the king's own ancestors or insulted his rivals by showing them to be unskilled or cowardly. Each scop improvised a personal version, emphasizing certain events according to his taste and ability, the audience, and the occasion.

According to the custom in most royal and noble courts, the scop could be called on at any time to deliver a tale, and in the long nights of winter these songs and poems could last for many hours. As the scops must have known, certain tales were more popular than others—they were guaranteed to grab and hold the attention of the toughest audience, the listeners who had heard it all many times before. *Beowulf* may represent a collection of "greatest hits," a weaving together of the poet's best-known stories, which reflect and contrast each other through the shared themes of heroism, selflessness, hope, and fate.

Among many other stories, the author of *Beowulf* included a story of the defeat of the Geats (Beowulf's people) by the Swedes and the death of the Geatish king Hygelac at the hands of the Franks. These stories recounted a glorious past, a time before the Anglo-Saxons arrived in Britain to conquer and settle the new land. They brought pride to their listeners in the same way that many semi-mythical tales and characters of the Wild West reflect the heroic pioneer days of the United States.

In translating a sung performance into the written word, according to critic W.J. Courthope, this poet gave important clues to his true calling. Unlike many critics of *Beowulf*,

Courthope sees *Beowulf* as a haphazard collection of traditional tales:

> The style of *Beowulf* is not that of a literary poet, but of a minstrel. Had it been a deliberate literary composition, it would have exhibited some traces of central design, and its joints and articulations would have been carefully marked; but the poem as it stands is a medley of heterogenous materials, singularly wanting in plan and consistency.... The poem, in its existing form, was composed for the purpose of chanting or recitation, on lines long familiar to the Teutonic race, and by the aid of materials derived perhaps from remote antiquity.[5]

Stylistic Clues to the Author of *Beowulf*

From the rhythm of the words and phrases, scholars have definitely agreed that *Beowulf* is a work of poetry, not prose. They have also been able to divide the prose of the manuscript into the 3,182 lines that make up the original poem. They largely agree that the style of the poem directly reflects

A thirteenth-century painting depicts a minstrel playing for a royal couple. Many scholars believe Beowulf *began as an oral tale sung for royalty.*

the style of sung poetry as it must have existed at the time of
Beowulf's composition.

Each line of *Beowulf* arrives in two parts, with an alliteration (similar sound) occurring in two words on either side of
the line. Rather than rhyming, this alliteration is the true
music of *Beowulf*, the source of invention that challenged the
author and delighted the audience. Scholar and critic J.R.R.
Tolkien, in an important essay entitled *"Beowulf:* The
Monsters and the Critics," describes how this method of
poetry worked:

> The very nature of Old English metre is often mis-
> judged. In it there is no single rhythmic pattern pro-
> gressing from the beginning of a line to the end, and
> repeated with variation in other lines. The lines do not
> go according to a tune. They are founded on a bal-
> ance; an opposition between two halves of roughly
> equivalent phonetic weight, and significant content,
> which are more often rhythmically contrasted than
> similar. They are more like masonry than music.[6]

To fill the framework of his story, the author of *Beowulf*
used familiar, formulaic phrases passed down by earlier generations of performers. This technique is as old as storytelling
itself and was used in the time of ancient Greece and in the
epics of Homer known to modern readers as the *Iliad*
and the *Odyssey*. Milman Perry, in his essay "The Homeric
Language as the Language of Oral Poetry," describes the
process as follows:

> When one singer...has hit upon a phrase which is
> pleasing and easily used, other singers will hear it, and
> then, when faced at the same (metrical) point in the
> line with the need of expressing the same idea, they
> will recall it and use it. If the phrase is so good poeti-
> cally and so useful metrically that it becomes in time

the one best way to express a certain idea in a given length of verse, and as such is passed on from one generation of poets to another, it has won a place for itself in the oral diction as a formula.[7]

Many formulas and stock phrases appear in *Beowulf*, as do the phrases known as kennings. A kenning is a metaphor, a short and poetic description of a person or place. The sea in *Beowulf* is called a "whale road" and a "swan road," God is known as the "Heavenly Shepherd" and the "Lord of Ages," the monster Grendel is called the "death shadow." To indicate a character, the poet also used epithets, such as "protector of Shieldings" for the Danish king Hrothgar, and genealogy, such as "son of Ecgtheow" for Beowulf.

The kennings and formulaic phrases of *Beowulf* reveal the author to have been an experienced storyteller, one who knew all the tricks to grabbing and holding the attention of an audience. The *Beowulf* poet shows all the skills of a professional entertainer, one well schooled in the tricks of his trade. These devices provide fascinating insights into the origins of poetry as oral performance—but they also make tough demands on a modern reader, who lives a great distance from the experience of the medieval Anglo-Saxons.

The Faith of the *Beowulf* Poet

Beowulf may indeed be a collection of old tales and legends—entertainments—dictated by a traditional court performer to a literate scribe. But most scholars also show that the story offers lessons for its audience and is meant to instruct as well as to entertain. The lessons of *Beowulf* are based on Christian ethics, a new philosophy in early medieval Britain, when questions of religion dominated literature and philosophy.

The seventh and eighth centuries were times of religious transformation in the Anglo-Saxon world. The old religion and the pagan pantheon of gods were vanishing, and the new faith

*Saint John from a page of the Lindisfarne Gospel, a seventh-century
Christian manuscript.* Beowulf *utilizes early Christian tales to develop its
characters and themes.*

of Christianity had arrived. When the Anglo-Saxon kings
accepted Christianity, they banished the old gods from their
religious observances and turned to the Christian god. But for
an evening's entertainment, they still assembled after a feast and
they still called on the scops for a good story from the old days.
The poets went to work, dutifully giving their stories a veneer
of Christian ethics and piety to make them more acceptable.

The author of *Beowulf*, says the critic William Witherle
Lawrence, had to adopt his story to the new ways:

Everything shows him to have been trained in the full technique of the professional poet. His heart was really in the pagan tales and traditions that had been celebrated for generations among his people by singers like himself. But, in the changed conditions of his time, he had to suppress all references to the old gods . . . and make over his pagans into good Christians.[8]

At various points in the poem, the *Beowulf* poet reveals his knowledge of biblical stories and lessons. While describing Grendel, the poet recounts how God exiled the race of monsters for a crime committed by Cain:

On the kindred of Cain He wreaked his vengeance
the eternal Lord, for his slaying of Abel.
Joyless to Cain was the feud; for the Maker
drove him afar from mankind for his crime.
Thence woke to being all broods of evil,
monsters and elves and spirits of darkness,
giants likewise, that for long days and dreary
warred against God; He paid them their wages.[9]

The poet also places words of Christian faith in the mouths of his characters—who belong to an entirely pagan world. In the following speech, Beowulf pledges to face the monster Grendel while unarmed. The poet replaces the old pagan notion of fate—the unknowable, inevitable train of future events—with a reference to God's will and judgment.

We shall refrain from
the sword in the night-time, if he durst challenge
to war without weapons; then God in his wisdom,
the holy Lord, to *him* adjudge the glory—
to which side so ever may seem meet to Him.[10]

Early in the poem, the author contrasts the Christian god's creation of light and earthly beauty with Grendel, a dark and destructive figure of pagan beliefs:

Then the bold spirit that abode in darkness
hardly with patience bore a bitter time—
hearing each day the din of rejoicing
loud in the hall, with the sound of the harp
and the scop's clear song. He that could tell us
of men's first beginings from far-past ages
declared that the Almighty fashioned the earth,
the bright-faced meadow encompassed with water,
and, rejoicing in might, did stablish [establish] the radiance
of sun and moon for light unto mortals,
and made rich and fair the regions of earth
with branches and leaves; life also he fashioned
for all kinds of creatures that live and move.[11]

Some critics of *Beowulf* believe that a devout Christian poet added these lines to *Beowulf* after it was originally written. In this way, a second author may have attempted to make the wholly pagan story acceptable to a Christian audience. But most historians believe *Beowulf* to be the work of a solitary

A ninth-century painting of Saint Gregory dictating to a scribe. Monks dictated oral tales such as Beowulf *to scribes to preserve them in written form.*

poet. They point out that there is no difference in poetic style or meter between these "Christian" lines and the rest of the poem. This poet may have been using an old pagan legend to praise the Christian god and to impart a lesson in Christian ethics and faith.

Like nearly all manuscripts of this time, the *Beowulf* manuscript was most probably created in a monastery, where books were produced in workshops known as scriptoria. The monks who lived within these monasteries sometimes enjoyed themselves with performances of songs and music from the outside secular world (although they were sometimes scolded for such entertainments by their more strictly religious superiors). The Christian themes of *Beowulf* would have made the poem worth preserving in written form. Critic Margaret E. Goldsmith supports the theory that the *Beowulf* poet was a member of a religious order:

> In view of the preservation of Beowulf in writing, there is a natural presumption that the poet was in some way connected with a religious house.... Some young men must have entered monasteries already proficient in this art, and the monks of that day were by no means enclosed within their walls; opportunities might well arise while journeying to listen to secular songs and tales, and even in the monastery itself diversions of the sort were not unknown.[12]

The religious outlook—both Christian and pagan—of *Beowulf's* creator remains a subject of hot debate among literary critics and scholars, as does the exact date of the original poem. To decide on exactly how old *Beowulf* is, historians can draw on many clues provided by the author—in the language used, and in historical names and events described in the poem. Because so little is actually known about these distant events, *Beowulf* is a valuable historical document as well as a work of poetic art.

CHAPTER TWO

The Historical Background of *Beowulf*

The action of *Beowulf* takes place well before the poet's time, in the semi-mythical, heroic past of Denmark, the ancient homeland of the Anglo-Saxons. The poet and his audience looked back to the great migrations that began in the days of the Roman Empire, when the Germanic tribes of northern Europe were frequently on the move and when warfare and rivalry among these tribes and nations were commonplace. They saw a glorious, epic tale in the conquest of Britain by their Anglo-Saxon forefathers. The figure of Beowulf epitomizes the valor of these ancestors, a hero who fights not only for personal glory and reward but also for the triumph of his nation. The heroics of Beowulf, the noble actions of the worthy king Hrothgar, the terrors of bloodthirsty monsters such as Grendel, and the vicissitudes of fate are all important themes of a poem that, like medieval life itself, does not promise a happy ending.

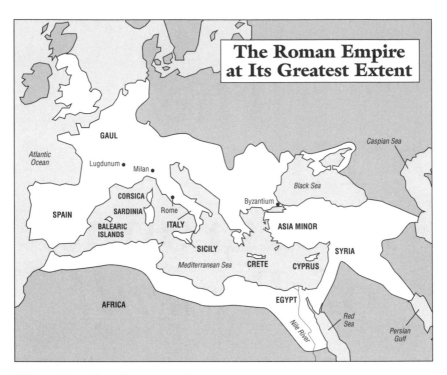

The Anglo-Saxon Conquest

The Anglo-Saxon migrations began when the Roman Empire still dominated southern and western Europe. In the time of the Roman emperor Julius Caesar, the first century B.C., the empire extended its frontiers as far north as the island of Britain. There, the Romans and the natives of the island, the Celtic people known as Britons, raised new towns. They also built two fortified walls across the windswept northern highlands in order to keep out the Scots and the Picts, warlike tribes of what is now Scotland who frequently raided Roman-governed lands to the south.

Distant from Rome, the imperial capital and center of power, the province had to defend itself against the raiders from the north by every means possible. This meant hiring mercenaries, known as federates, who sailed from their homeland in what is now northern Germany to fight under Roman authority. The British and Romans knew these mercenaries as

"Saxons," although several other tribes may have been involved, including Angles, Frisians, Jutes, and Danes.

By the fifth century A.D. Roman power in Britain had grown weak, and by the end of that century the Western Roman Empire had collapsed. The Roman armies and government disappeared, but the federates remained. Living in a land more fertile than their original homes, they invited fellow tribesmen from the continent to settle in Britain.

These events began the Anglo-Saxon settlement of Britain. For many years after the Roman collapse, the Germanic armies fought with the native Britons for mastery of the island; eventually the Anglo-Saxons prevailed, driving the Britons into the mountains and the remote coastal regions of western Britain. The Anglo-Saxons divided their new territory into several small kingdoms, known to historians as the heptarchy (seven kingdoms). The tribe of Angles settled in the lowlands of eastern Britain and eventually gave their name to the kingdom, unified much later, and known as England.

The Coming of Christianity

The pagan Anglo-Saxons embraced a pantheon of anthropomorphic (humanlike) gods—including Odin, Freya, and Thor—that represented the elemental forces of nature. These gods had originated among the Germanic peoples of northern Europe and Scandinavia. Since arriving on the island of Britain, the Anglo-Saxons raised pagan temples on hilltops and in forest groves and made sacrifices, both animal and human, to their favored deities.

A new faith arrived on their island in the year 597 with the Christian missionary Augustine, who came on the instructions of Pope Gregory I. Augustine landed in Kent, in southeastern England, and quickly converted the king of that realm, Aethelberht, to Christianity. The missionaries then converted the rulers of two other small kingdoms, Essex and East Anglia. Later, a Christian chaplain, Paulinus, baptized Edwin, the king of Northumbria and the son-in-law of Aethelberht.

The Christians built churches, often on the site of old pagan temples, and established bishops in the towns of Canterbury, Rochester, London, and York.

By the eighth century paganism had largely disappeared. Anglo-Saxon leaders seeking any advantage they might gain over rival tribes saw in the Christian church a powerful ally. To the pagans of Britain, the missionaries brought not only a new faith but also a new kind of civilization. As described by James W. Earl, "The conversion [of the pagan Anglo-Saxons] was relatively rapid, native religion was largely eradicated, and letters, laws, and the other arts of Christian civilization were introduced. Within only a century, the Anglo-Saxons entered into a golden age of Christian learning and international influence, sending their own missionaries and scholars into a declining Europe."[13]

One of the most important arts brought by the Christian missionaries to England was a new method of communication: writing. Using ink and parchment, monks and scribes could set down, in a permanent form, the Bible, the word of the Christian god. They could write about the lives of the Christian saints, explain biblical stories and passages, and give instruction on the proper ways to observe Christian holidays and feasts. They could record their own history. The Venerable Bede, a monk of the monastery of Jarrow in Northumbria, described the recent history and the conversion of England in his manuscript *The History of the English Church and People*, a work that dates to the year 731.

Most historians believe that it was during Bede's time that *Beowulf* was also composed. There is little doubt that the poem is the work of a Christian, someone who holds strongly to the new faith and who believes fervently in the Christian god. Yet *Beowulf* is also the work of someone who holds great admiration for the pagan past of his ancestors. The author looks back on his cast of characters, on their sense of honor and their courage in battle, and on the great rivalries in which they fought and died, with nostalgia.

In *Beowulf*, Christian piety is often mixed with old pagan beliefs and imagery:

> But God had vouchsafed them
> the weavings of victory—to the folk of the Weders,
> solace and support, that they all should triumph
> over their foemen through one man's might,
> through his own great strength; the truth is made known
> that God in His might forever hath governed
> the race of mankind.[14]

The author reveals within his story the workings of fate, the inevitable, unknowable end that the pagan Germans believed all people must fulfill. In the lines of *Beowulf*, this ancient pagan concept of fate is given a veneer of Christian piety. God, says the author of *Beowulf*, is the one who in the end will determine fate. To give this idea more power, the author applies it to tribes, kings, and heroes who really existed and whose stories were well known to his audience.

History and *Beowulf*

Beowulf describes three important tribes of pagan Scandinavia: the Danes, who lived in the peninsula of Jutland, in what is now modern Denmark; the Geats, a people of what is now southern Sweden; and the Swedes, who lived to the north of the Geats. In his essay "Teaching the Backgrounds," Fred C. Robinson explains how the poet of *Beowulf* turned the true history of the Geats into an epic story:

> In *Beowulf* we read of much strife between the Geatas [Geats] and the Swedes, and Scandinavian records verify both the conflicts of the Swedes at this time and the names of their rulers. . . . The records are not specific about the role the Geatas play in these wars or about their ultimate fate, but the speakers in the poem are very specific about the fate of the Geatas: Wiglaf, the messenger, and the woman mourning at Beowulf's funeral all agree that the

nation faces disaster once King Beowulf is dead. Knowing the dismal future that history holds for the Geatas enables us to complete the poem's tragic meaning: heroic splendor and the values of the pre-Christian world are unavailing before the destructive forces of a brutal age.[15]

Certain persons mentioned in *Beowulf* did exist and enjoyed heroic reputations long after their deaths among the poets and audiences of Anglo-Saxon England. The poet makes the historical Hygelac, a king of the Geats, the uncle of Beowulf. The real Hygelac was a Scandinavian king who was best known for a failed attack on the coasts of northwestern Europe during the early sixth century. Raiding on the Franks, the Frisians, and the Hetware, Hygelac was following an old tradition among the Scandinavians, who found fruitful grounds for their piracy and raiding in the warmer and more productive lands of continental Europe. Hygelac's raid ended in his own death in about the year 516 A.D. The final conquest of his people, the Geats, by the Swedes took place some time later in the sixth century—after which the Geats completely disappeared from written historical records.

These events may have been the original inspiration for *Beowulf*. Hygelac is the Geatish king whom Beowulf serves faithfully, and the poem recounts Hygelac's raid and places Beowulf in the thick of the action:

> Nor was that the least
> of hand-to-hand combats where Higelac [Hygelac]
> was slain,
> when the king of the Geats, the gracious prince of peoples,
> Hrethel's son, fell 'mid the storms of battle
> in Frisian lands by the thirsty sword,
> smitten by the steel; thence came Beowulf
> by his own strength, achieving a swimming feat.
> Thirty battle-coats on his arm he bore,
> on his single arm, when to sea he went down.[16]

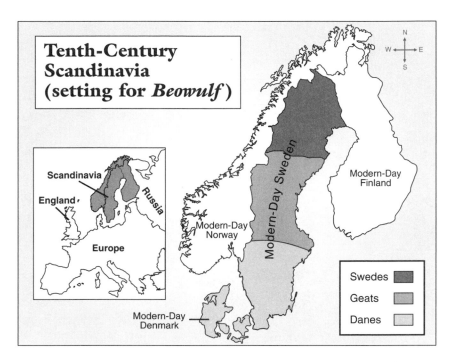

Tenth-Century
Scandinavia
(setting for *Beowulf*)

Scandinavia

England

Europe

Russia

Modern-Day
Norway

Modern-Day Sweden

Modern-Day
Finland

Modern-Day
Denmark

Swedes
Geats
Danes

Old Scandinavian poetry also describes Scyld Scefing, a legendary king of the Danes. Scyld appears in the first lines of *Beowulf* as the founder of the Scylding dynasty. The name *Scyld* means "Shield" or "Protector," and according to the legends, this king defeated a rival tribe, the Heruli, and made the Danes the most powerful tribe in the Jutland peninsula that is now a part of modern Denmark.

Like Hygelac and Scyld, Hrothgar, a member of the Scylding dynasty, also existed. Hrothgar ruled Denmark from a royal hall, and historians locate one such structure at the site of the modern village of Leire in Denmark. According to the medieval historian Saxo Grammaticus, the Danish royal family was thrown into turmoil after the death of Hrothgar when his brother Hrothulf killed Hrethric, the son of Hrothgar and Queen Wealhtheow, and seized the throne for himself.

This event was probably known to the poet of *Beowulf*, who, in the poem, has Hrothgar's queen, Wealhtheow, speak the following ironic words of hope to Beowulf:

Danish soldiers land on the Northumbrian coast of England to conduct a raid in 870. Beowulf *uses the Danes and their history of warfare to develop its plot.*

Well do I know
my gracious Hrothulf, that he will govern
the youth in honour, if thou first before him,
Lord of the Scyldings, leavest the world;
I ween [imagine] that with good he will duly requite
our offspring, remembering all the favours
we both have shown him in days gone by,
while he was a child, for his pleasure and honour.[17]

With this ironic passage, the *Beowulf* poet creates a tense expectancy within his audience, who knew that the real Hrothulf did not, in fact, use the young ones well—instead, he usurped their position and authority, committing murder in the process. This audience also probably knew of the war between the Danes and the Heathobards, which the character of Beowulf predicts as a future event in the poem. In the poem, Hrothgar offers his daughter Freawaru in marriage to Ingeld, the king of the Heathobards, in hopes that this marriage will heal a long-standing feud between the Danes and the Heathobards.

But old resentments and wrongs die hard in the world of the pagan Germans. It is a point of honor to revenge the death of a kinsman, a lord, or a fellow warrior, and a mere wedding does not forestall the need for this revenge. The *Beowulf* poet brings this out in a "story within a story," an account of Ingeld and Freawaru's wedding feast. During the feast, a grief-stricken Heathobard warrior takes offense at the swagger of the Danes who have joined them in the hall:

The restless spirit
would not stay in the breast. The hall was decorated
with the lives of the foe, a tapestry of blood,
Finn slain too, the king with his troop,
and the queen taken.[18]

The war between the Danes and the Heathobards begins anew, and the cycle of killing and revenge resumes. To the

Beowulf poet and his audience, this was all recent history—everyday life in the time of the migrations, when the only law of the land was the bond of honor between warriors and their overlords, and justice belonged in the hands of the individual, not the state.

Historians are unsure if Beowulf himself stands in for a historical character. In his book *"Beowulf" and Epic Tradition*, the writer William Witherle Lawrence points out that the poet of *Beowulf* provides little in the way of precise detail concerning this figure:

> Whether he was confused or identified with some figure in the Geat royal house, whose position he occupied, and whose name was supplanted by his own, we do not know. It appears unlikely, however, that this was the case. If it did actually happen, most of the attributes of the figure in question were lost in the process of amalgamation. Beowulf was, to be sure, given a father named Ecgtheow...who may have been historical, and he was further identified with the Geatic clan of the Waegmundingas, which was probably historical.... The story in its late Anglo-Saxon form...while avowedly presenting Beowulf as an ideal Germanic prince, really gives precise information only in regard to his supernatural adventures.[19]

Despite whether he was based on a historical person, the character of Beowulf endured as an archetype in English society and literature, as essayist Sarah F. McNary notes:

> Though Beowulf, as a single concrete character, passed so early out of English thought, the elements of his being passed into the English people, and he lives today in enduring qualities. He appears in history and in literature in varied forms. He lives the free life of law-abiding lawlessness with Robin Hood in Sherwood Forest....Was his struggle with the dragons all in vain, when a dragon-slayer [St. George] is

A twelfth-century painting depicts an Anglo-Saxon king being captured by the Danes. Such acts of war prompt tales of revenge which are central to the story of Beowulf.

patron saint of England? If Beowulf is no longer an ideal in the higher sense, it is because he has been lived into a type.[20]

In this way, the hero of *Beowulf* survives, although steeped in legend. The selfless hero, who fights and wins against impossible odds, who is let down by his own people, and who endures in memory after his death, is present in numberless poems, novels, plays, and movies up to the twenty-first century. This strong connection to the literature that would follow makes *Beowulf* a fascinating work of literature, one that will continue to beguile readers, frustrate students, and inspire new translations and scholarly debates for a long time to come.

CHAPTER THREE

The Story of *Beowulf*

The *Beowulf* poet writes of the heroic deeds of a noble warrior of the Geats. This warrior, Beowulf, fights at first simply for the glory and honor that comes with victory in single combat against supernatural enemies. But after becoming the ruler of his people, he fights to protect his own nation from the righteous vengeance of a treasure-hoarding dragon. Beowulf is defeated and killed, and his memory is honored by those who survive him.

The Scylding Dynasty

The *Beowulf* poet begins his tale by describing Scyld Scefing, the founder of the Scylding dynasty, who reigned honorably among the Danes. When Scyld dies, his people honor him with a royal funeral, setting him adrift in the hold of a mighty warship laden with treasure—weapons, coats of mail, and a gold standard raised above his head. The Danes cast his funeral ship adrift to land on a distant, unknown shore.

The Scylding dynasty continues with Scyld's son Beowulf (not the Beowulf of the poem's title), and then with his grandson Halfdane. Halfdane has four children: three sons, Heorogar, Hrothgar, and Halga; and a daughter, who becomes the queen of the Swedish ruler Onela. Hrothgar rules the Danes after the death of his father.

Hrothgar's royal mead hall, Heorot, is a wonder of the world, a place where Hrothgar's knights and retainers live in comradely warmth and where long evenings are spent in drinking, feasting, storytelling, and other entertainments. The king freely rewards his loyal followers, and his reputation for generosity earns him the nickname of "ring giver."

The mead hall is the center of Hrothgar's royal power. There, poets and singers celebrate the exploits of the king and of his ancestors. But the warmth and liveliness of the hall make a determined enemy out of Grendel, a jealous monster who lives in a lake within earshot of the voices and singing of Heorot. The pleasant sound of a harp is unbearable to Grendel, a monster descended from the biblical Cain, who murdered his own brother and whose brood of monsters and ghosts were condemned as eternal outcasts by God.

The Ravages of Grendel

One night, after a long bout of drinking, Hrothgar's knights slumber within the walls of Heorot. Grendel sneaks into the hall and massacres thirty Danes, returning to his lair to feast on their bodies. The next morning Hrothgar and the other survivors awake to find the terrifying trail of death and blood left behind by Grendel. Not satisfied with the carnage he has brought to Heorot, Grendel returns the next night. For the next twelve years, Grendel casts his frightening shadow over Heorot, and voices of merriment are stilled. The knights and retainers of Hrothgar wisely flee the hall and settle elsewhere, and the king becomes a powerless, frightened, and embittered old man. Hrothgar's counselors give him plenty of advice, and the Danes make many offerings at their pagan shrines, but all to no avail.

Sad songs about the fate of Heorot are sung far and wide. Among the Geats, a people living near the Danes, a prince named Beowulf hears of Grendel and of the terror the monster has brought to the hall of Heorot. A man of extraordinary

The hideous Grendel carries off the knights of Hrothgar. This act brings the hero Beowulf to Heorot to stop the murderous monster.

strength and fighting prowess, Beowulf is a loyal thane, or retainer, of Hygelac, the king of the Geats. In quest of glory and reward, Beowulf selects fourteen of the strongest and most loyal knights of Geatland and prepares to sail for Denmark. No one among the Geats tries to stop him, and the omens all seem to predict his victory.

Beowulf sets sail with his eager followers. On landing along the rugged coast of Denmark, the group meets a watchman, who challenges these unexpected strangers. Beowulf boasts that he is the son of a noble warrior named Ecgtheow and then reveals his mission to save Hrothgar and his court from the bloodthirsty Grendel. Impressed with Beowulf's proud and imposing presence, the watchman offers to guide them to Heorot.

Beowulf and the Geats march to Heorot, their mail and weapons gleaming and their iron armor ringing. When they arrive there, they stack their wooden shields against a wall and rest on benches. A messenger named Wulfgar, a chief of the friendly tribe of Wendels, approaches them and demands to hear the reason for their coming. Beowulf asks to speak directly to the king, and Wulfgar agrees to bring the news of the Geats' arrival to Hrothgar.

Wulfgar speaks well of the Geats to Hrothgar, reporting that the strangers seem worthy of the king's respect. Hrothgar recalls Beowulf as a much younger man and as the son of Ecgtheow, who was married to the daughter of Hrethel the Geat. Beowulf, so Hrothgar has heard, is a warrior of great strength. Hrothgar decides to admit Beowulf into Heorot. The Geats are allowed to approach the king in their helmets and armor, but as a token of their friendly intentions, they must first set aside their shields and spears.

Beowulf Fights Grendel

Beowulf meets with Hrothgar and recounts the adventures of his youth, his battles with sea beasts, and his triumphs against the enemies of the Geats. The prince then pledges to fight and defeat Grendel in hand-to-hand combat without the use of weapons. Beowulf declares that the outcome will be determined by God and asks only that if he is killed, the Danes return his chain mail shirt to King Hygelac, his lord and master in Geatland.

Hrothgar eagerly accepts Beowulf's offer to rid Heorot of the monster. He recalls the feud between Beowulf's father,

Ecgtheow, and the Wulfing clan. Forced to take refuge among the Danes, Ecgtheow was helped by Hrothgar, who sent a ransom to the Wulfings to settle the feud, after which Ecgtheow swore allegiance to Hrothgar. Thus, Beowulf and Hrothgar revive an old bond.

Hrothgar orders the benches of Heorot cleared for Beowulf's men. The servants pour mead, and a minstrel sings for the entertainment of the Geats. But not all of the Danes feel delight and relief at Beowulf's arrival. One of Hrothgar's knights, Unferth, looks on the Geatish prince with jealousy. He challenges Beowulf by claiming that one of Beowulf's famous deeds—a swimming contest with a friend named Breca—was done only out of vanity and that Breca, in fact, defeated Beowulf in this contest. In the same way, Unferth promises, Beowulf will be defeated by the monster.

Beowulf gives a strong retort. He claims that Unferth is letting his beer do the talking, and then he explains that he slew nine sea monsters during the race with Breca. In fact, Beowulf and Breca had been friends since childhood and had often challenged each other with these contests of strength and stamina. Beowulf then silences Unferth with some criticism of his own, pointing out that Unferth's only notable deed was the slaying of his own brother, a deed for which Unferth will pay by suffering eternal damnation in the depths of Hell.

Unferth falls silent, and the company resumes its drinking and merrymaking. Wealhtheow, Hrothgar's queen, sees to it that the guests are well supplied with food and drink. She offers the mead cup first to Hrothgar, the lord of Heorot, then to Beowulf, welcoming the prince to the hall and thanking God for answering her prayers for deliverance from Grendel.

The knights of Heorot retire to their beds, and Hrothgar appoints Beowulf as the master (lord) of the hall—the first time in his life that the king has ever allowed anyone to reign over the hall in his place. While the other guardians of Heorot slumber, Beowulf prepares to meet Grendel in combat.

Soon afterward Grendel arrives, ripping the doors of Heorot from their hinges and setting to his bloody work. He kills and eats one of the sleeping knights but then feels Beowulf's mighty grasp. The monster panics and tries to flee the hall, but Beowulf tears Grendel's hand and arm from his body. The sound of their combat rings through Heorot. Benches are smashed and a terrifying wail is heard. Awakened by the tumult, Beowulf's companions strike at the monster

Beowulf rips off Grendel's arm, killing him and ending the monster's reign of terror in Heorot.

with their swords. They do not realize that ordinary weapons are useless against the monster, who has cast a spell on the sharp edges of his enemies' swords. Grendel finally escapes back to his lair, where he dies of the wounds inflicted by Beowulf. As a trophy of the battle, Beowulf hangs Grendel's bloody limb up on the wall of Heorot.

The Celebration Feast

Clans from far and wide come to Heorot to wonder at the huge footprints left by the monster, who had dived deep into his lair, leaving a wake of blood and gore on the waters of his marsh den. At a feast to celebrate Beowulf's victory, a singer, one of Hrothgar's thanes, recites the tale of Sigemund, another famous dragon slayer.

Arriving in the hall, attended by his queen, Hrothgar sings the praises of Beowulf. In the view of Hrothgar and the Danes, Beowulf has been sent by the grace of God, and with the Lord's assistance he has accomplished something that the Danes, for all their strength and valor, never could. The king then adopts Beowulf as his son. Beowulf recalls the fight with Grendel and how he pinned the monster, who nevertheless managed to retreat to his lair, where he would die of the wounds inflicted on him. Seeing the monster's hand and arm on the wall of Heorot, the admiring Unferth forgets his envy of Beowulf.

The Danes then set to repairing the hall, which has been wrecked by the mighty struggle of the night before. Hrothgar and his followers sit down to feast, and the king rewards Beowulf with a gold standard, a helmet, and a suit of chain mail as well as a sword and eight fine warhorses, each sporting a golden bridle. Each of Beowulf's men also receives a reward.

A court poet then recites another heroic song, the tragic story of Finn, the king of the Frisians. The Danish princess Hildeburh had married Finn, but this did not prevent the Danish chief Hengest from mounting an attack on his old

Frisian enemies. After much bloodshed, the two sides called a truce. Finn allowed the Danes to share his hall, where Hengest and the Danes would receive tribute from Finn—gifts in the same measure he would give his own Frisians. Hildeburh had to lament the death of her own son and brother in the fight between the Danes and the Frisians, but through a long and bitter winter Hengest could not forget the deaths of his comrades. Swearing vengeance, the Danes ambushed and killed Finn, ransacked Finn's hall, and brought Hildeburh and a Frisian treasure back to Denmark.

Grendel's Mother Swears Revenge

After the story of Finn ends, Hrothgar's queen, Wealhtheow, joins the company. Wealhtheow fervently hopes that Hrothulf, the brother of Hrothgar, will act justly toward her two sons, Hrethric and Hrothmund, if Hrothulf should inherit the throne of Denmark. She also wishes for peace between the Geats and the Danes, although she knows that between these two neighboring peoples the chance of strife and warfare will be ever present.

The Danes present Beowulf with more gifts: arm rings, a shirt of chain mail, rings, and a golden torque, or collar. The poet of *Beowulf* then reveals that on a fateful future day, King Hygelac of the Geats will wear this torque during a raid on the powerful Frisians and suffer a warrior's death at their hands.

In the meantime, as the Danes prepare for sleep and the guards of Heorot take their posts, the mother of Grendel lurks outside seeking revenge for her son's death. She enters the hall and captures Aeschere, one of Hrothgar's favorite knights, and steals Grendel's bloody limb. Fleeing at the sight of Danish warriors preparing to attack, she retires to her lair and prepares to make a meal of Aeschere.

Hrothgar bitterly laments the loss of his trusted knight. The Danes summon Beowulf, who had been resting in another lodging. Hrothgar tells Beowulf of the attack and the death of Aeschere. He describes the mere, a black pool of

Beowulf and the Danes come upon the head of Aeschere in front of the watery lair of Grendel's mother.

water where the unseen depths shelter monsters that ravage the nearby countryside. Hrothgar asks for Beowulf's help, and Beowulf calms the king with encouraging words and a promise to kill Grendel's mother.

The Danes follow the trail of Grendel's mother and find the head of Aeschere at the foot of a cliff, where gore and blood wallow up from a black pool of water. Reptiles swim in the water, and monsters crowd the nearby slopes. Beowulf kills one of the monsters with an arrow and then prepares for battle by donning his chain mail, his golden helmet, and an ancient sword named Hrunting, lent to him by Unferth. Beowulf speaks to Hrothgar, asking again that the Danes honor him if he should die by sending his treasure home to Hygelac. Beowulf also pledges his own sword to Unferth, to return Unferth's offer of Hrunting.

Beowulf plunges into the water and swims nearly an entire day to reach the bottom. Beset by monsters and by Grendel's mother, he swings Hrunting at the body of Grendel's mother—with no effect. The two begin to grapple; the monster pulls out a broad knife, but Beowulf's body armor protects him from the blow. Seeing a giant's sword hanging on the wall of the cave, Beowulf takes the weapon and slashes at the monster's neck, toppling her to the floor with a mortal blow.

A shaft of light then illuminates the cave and the body of the slain Grendel. To take further vengeance for all the murders committed by Grendel, Beowulf strikes off the dead monster's head. A great cloud of blood rises to the surface of the lake. Those waiting on the shore fear the worst: the death of Beowulf by the claws of Grendel's mother. The Danes retreat from the lake in fear of more attacks on their hall, but Beowulf's Geat companions remain behind.

Their patience is rewarded when Beowulf appears alive and well and carrying the head of Grendel and the hilt of the monster's sword, whose blade was melted by the blood of Grendel's mother. The Geats hoist the head of Grendel high on a spear and bring it to the hall of Heorot. While Hrothgar's queen and company stare at the trophy in awe and horror, Beowulf recounts his valiant fight against Grendel's mother.

Beowulf Returns to the Land of the Geats

Beowulf presents the giant's sword hilt to Hrothgar, who praises the prince and then speaks of the bad king Heremod, who, in contrast to the noble Beowulf, brought only grief to the Danes. Hrothgar warns Beowulf of the dangers of fame and power and how many men have been led astray by their own pride and unchecked desires. Hrothgar tells of his own long reign over the Danes and how he deceived himself into thinking that his enemies had been permanently vanquished. Hrothgar warns Beowulf against covetousness and pride, faults that have brought about the sad end of many a noble warrior.

The next morning Beowulf returns Hrunting to Unferth and prepares to take his leave of Hrothgar. But while saying farewell and inviting his guest to return, Hrothgar has a frightening premonition: He will never again meet Beowulf face to face. Saluted by the watchman who had seen them arrive on the shore, the Geats set sail in a boat laden with gifts from the grateful Danes.

Beowulf returns to his homeland, where the news of his exploits has preceded him. Queen Hygd is prepared to meet the company of heroes, and although still a young woman, she is thoughtful and generous to the thanes of Hygelac— much the opposite of the evil Queen Modthryth, a former queen of the Geats who would bind, torture, and murder any thane who had the nerve to look her in the eye.

Questioned intently by the curious Hygelac, Beowulf tells of his adventures and his battles to the Geats assembled at the royal court. At Hrothgar's court, as he recalls, he saw the gracious Freawaru, the king's daughter, who had been pledged in marriage to Ingeld, lord of the Heathobards. Beowulf fears that this marriage alliance will not settle the bad blood between the Danes and Heathobards, however, and predicts a fight between the two sides at the wedding feast.

Beowulf then describes his fight with Grendel and Grendel's mother, and he presents the gifts of the Danes to his uncle Hygelac: the gold standard, the helmet, the shirt of mail, the sword, and four horses. Hygelac returns the favor by presenting Beowulf with a gem-studded sword and a generous grant of land, in which Beowulf would have his own hall and throne.

The Reign of Beowulf

King Hygelac's reign ends with his death during a raid on Frisia, a land on the distant coast of Europe. Hygelac is succeeded by his son Heardred, even though the widow of

Hygelac, Queen Hygd, knows that Beowulf would make the better king. On the death of Heardred in battle with the Swedes, Beowulf ascends the throne of the Geats. Beowulf's long and peaceful reign of fifty years is marked by his skillful diplomacy, which allows the Geats to escape the trials and tribulations of constant warfare.

But the Geats are troubled in Beowulf's old age by the rampages of an angry dragon. The protector of a treasure hoard left behind by the last survivor of a vanished race, the dragon vowed revenge when a slave managed to steal a golden cup. By stealing the cup and presenting it to his master, the slave sought to win a pardon for his own past wrongs.

Hunting for the thief, the enraged dragon leaves his lair by night and burns everything in his path, even the home of Beowulf and the throne of the Geats. His mind anguished at the destruction wrought among his countrymen, the aging Beowulf once again prepares to do battle with a supernatural monster. There seems little to fear; Beowulf has defeated monsters before. He had accomplished his last great deed during Hygelac's raid on the Frisians when, after the death of Hygelac, Beowulf had swum a great distance home while weighed down with a great treasure hoard captured in battle.

The poet travels back in time to recall how Queen Hygd had asked Beowulf to take the Geatish throne after the death of Hygelac. But Beowulf, a man of honor, had refused to supercede the rightful heir, Heardred. As it turned out, the queen's fears were justified; Heardred had foolishly given shelter to the two sons of Ohthere, who had rebelled against their lords in Sweden. For his pains, Heardred was killed, to be succeeded by King Beowulf, who then settled the feud among the Swedes himself.

To deal with the fire-breathing dragon, the king now selects a company of eleven brave warriors to assist him and orders the making of a strong iron shield. He also forces the reluctant thief to accompany him as a guide.

Beowulf's Final Battle

Beowulf approaches the dragon's lair and prepares for battle by telling the story of his life to his companions. He had been taken in as a ward by Hrethel, king of the Geats and the father of Hygelac. Hrethel had suffered deeply when his son Herebeald was accidentally killed by an arrow shot by Herebeald's brother Haethcyn. Because the killing was between brothers, there was no way to pay the blood money, the pay-

Using his shield for protection against the dragon's fiery breath, Beowulf raises his sword to slay the dragon in his final heroic battle.

ment made to a victim's family to atone for his killing, in accordance with the custom of the Geats and Danes. Justice could not be served, and so this terrible act was the undoing of the old king, who spent the rest of his days lamenting the unavenged death of his son.

The death of Hrethel brought fighting between the Geats and their rivals, the Swedes. During this fighting Haethcyn was killed, as was the Swedish king, Ongentheow, who was laid low by a blow from the sword of Eofor, a knight in the service of Hygelac. Beowulf recalls that he had always fought at the front of the line for Hygelac, who rewarded this loyalty with many lavish gifts. Just as Beowulf had once killed Dayraven the Frank with his bare hands, he now promises to destroy the treasure-hoarding dragon.

Beowulf tells his followers to stand aside, as this fight is his and his alone. He enters the dragon's lair and shouts out an angry challenge to his nemesis. While the hot fires of the dragon's breath surround him, Beowulf raises his shield and strikes a glancing blow at the beast with his sword. The sword fails him and only enrages the dragon, whose flames drive away the other frightened warriors, except for Wiglaf—the only man courageous enough to stand by the king in his hour of peril.

While the dragon grasps Beowulf, Wiglaf raises his own sword, which had once belonged to Eanmund, a man slain by Wiglaf's father, Weohstan. With this ancient blade, Wiglaf deals the creature a strong blow. When the dragon chars Wiglaf's shield to cinders, Beowulf offers the protection of his own and then strikes the dragon with his sword—which snaps from Beowulf's own sheer strength.

The fallen Beowulf lies beside the dead dragon as Wiglaf brings the dragon's hoard to be placed on the funeral pyre.

The dragon clamps his sharp fangs into the neck of Beowulf, whose body runs wet with blood. Wiglaf delivers a fatal thrust of his sword into the belly of the dragon and then turns to Beowulf to comfort the dying king. Wiglaf washes the wounds of Beowulf, who asks Wiglaf to go see the dragon's hoard for himself. Wiglaf brings some of the dragon's treasure before Beowulf, who thanks his loyal companion and asks him to justly rule the Geats after his death. Beowulf rewards Wiglaf with the gift of his own golden collar, helmet, harness, and arm ring.

After the king dies, the ten timid warriors return, walking behind their shields, to the scene. Wiglaf berates them for their cowardice. His actions at this battle will bring Wiglaf the title of king of the Geats, but Wiglaf knows that the cowardice of these thanes, who had been so well rewarded by Beowulf over the years for their service, will soon become known to their enemies and will doom the Geat nation to an ignoble defeat.

Beowulf had given instructions for his funeral and had asked that a mound be raised to hold the dragon's treasure. But the poet describes the treasure as cursed by those who buried it, and declares that God would only permit someone pleasing to him to open the hoard.

A messenger brings the news of Beowulf's death back to the Geats. Now that the king is dead, the messenger announces, the Geats will surely be conquered by the Swedes. Beowulf is burned on a magnificent funeral pyre. Under Wiglaf's direction, the Geats enter the dragon's barrow, find the dragon's corpse, and pitch it over a sea cliff. They build the mound that will hold their king's remains and the cursed treasure hoard. As the smoke and flames billow over Beowulf's funeral pyre, a woman recites a sad lament for Beowulf. This is followed by a dirge sung by twelve champions on horseback, who slowly circle the tomb and sing the glories of their dead king.

CHAPTER FOUR

The Cast of Characters

From contemporary histories of the early Middle Ages, historians know that some of the characters in *Beowulf* actually existed. Others are probably fictional, and some—such as the monsters and the dragon—are fantasy. For many years critics of the poem have enjoyed lively debate over the actual identity of the characters in *Beowulf*, approaching the poem like a tangled mystery that can never be completely solved. The tangled cast can be mysterious and downright frustrating to the reader, who must keep track of Danes, Geats, and others who play some role in the hero's adventures.

Beowulf

Beowulf, whose name historians believe means "Son of the Bear," is a prince of the Geats, a Germanic tribe that lived in what is now southern Sweden. He is the son of the noble warrior Ecgtheow, and his mother was the daughter of Hrethel the Geat. Beowulf lives in the service of his uncle Hygelac, the king of the Geats, yet under Hygelac's peaceful reign his opportunities for battle, and for honor and glory, are limited. For this reason, he brings fifteen companions to the court of King Hrothgar and the Danes to slay Grendel, the demon who for twelve years has menaced the king and his court at the hall of Heorot. Beowulf vows to slay the monster or die trying.

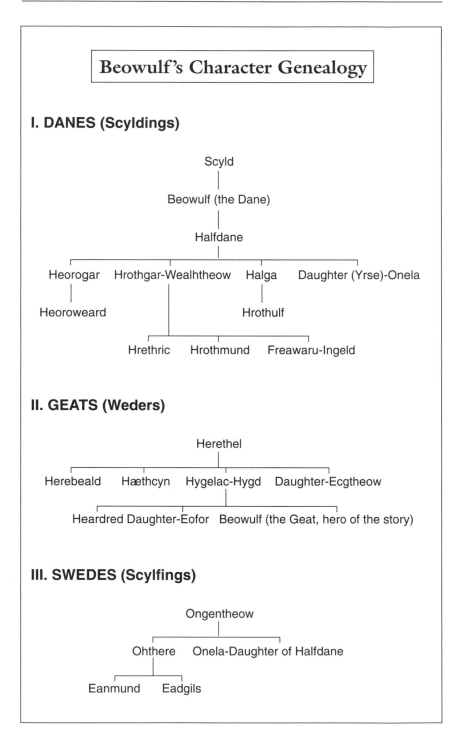

Beowulf's Character Genealogy

I. DANES (Scyldings)

Scyld

Beowulf (the Dane)

Halfdane

Heorogar — Hrothgar-Wealhtheow — Halga — Daughter (Yrse)-Onela

Heoroweard — Hrothulf

Hrethric — Hrothmund — Freawaru-Ingeld

II. GEATS (Weders)

Herethel

Herebeald — Hæthcyn — Hygelac-Hygd — Daughter-Ecgtheow

Heardred Daughter-Eofor — Beowulf (the Geat, hero of the story)

III. SWEDES (Scylfings)

Ongentheow

Ohthere — Onela-Daughter of Halfdane

Eanmund — Eadgils

Beowulf has the strength of thirty men and is fearsome in single combat. He likes nothing better than a test of his courage and skill and eagerly accepts challenges whether they come from friend or foe. Yet he is also magnanimous to his enemies, with a keen sense of fairness and justice. He has all the attributes, and more, of a noble warrior; for the original audience of the poem, he represents all that is good in a leader:

> Thus Beowulf bore himself with valour;
> he was formidable in battle yet behaved with honour
> and took no advantage; never cut down
> a comrade who was drunk, kept his temper
> and, warrior that he was, watched and controlled
> his God-sent strength and his outstanding
> natural powers.[21]

Beowulf comes to the aid of the Danes in their royal hall of Heorot. He slays Grendel in single combat, using nothing more than the powerful grip of his hands. Beowulf then kills Grendel's mother after she attempts to avenge her son by coming to Heorot and making off with Hrothgar's favorite thane. After this second victory, Beowulf becomes king of the Geats and reigns fifty years before his own death in combat with a dragon.

Beowulf possesses not only the attributes of a warrior but also those of a king: wisdom, restraint, and generosity. When Unferth the Dane mocks Beowulf, belittling his prowess, Beowulf quiets the jealous man not by fighting and killing him but rather by pointing out Unferth's own shortcomings. During Beowulf's reign over the Geats, the nation enjoys peace and prosperity, the result of Beowulf's settling of the feud that killed his predecessor, Heardred.

As a king, Beowulf also has a strong sense of duty to his nation. When the Geats are threatened by the jealous, treasure-hoarding dragon, Beowulf accepts the challenge without hesitation. The poet foreshadows Beowulf's death in combat with the dragon, illustrating the old pagan belief in fate, or the belief that every person's life and death has been determined beforehand and all of his or her actions will eventually fulfill this fate. No matter how strong or wise Beowulf is, he cannot escape his fate—although it remains unknown to him until the moment of his passing.

The Dragon

The last of the beasts to be faced by Beowulf, the dragon is a serpentine creature, fifty feet long, with a pair of wings, a red-hot breath of fire, and a fatal bite. The dragon guards a great treasure that has been buried on a solitary hill for three hundred years. When a thief steals a golden cup from the hoard, the dragon vows revenge and rains fire and death down on the Geats. To end this menace, Beowulf once again takes up his sword and his shield and prepares to do battle with the supernatural.

Although Beowulf is the mightiest of the Geats and has already proved his mettle in his fights with Grendel and Grendel's mother, he finds a deadly opponent in the dragon, who spits out a fire so terrifying that it sends all of Beowulf's handpicked companions (except for Wiglaf) fleeing for their lives. During the battle the dragon sinks his poisonous fangs into Beowulf's neck, but it is in turn dealt a fatal blow by Wiglaf. Finally, the dying Beowulf cuts the dragon in two. On Beowulf's instructions, the treasure hoard is brought out of the dragon's lair, but because it carries a curse, no man can possess it. Instead, it is buried with Beowulf in his funeral mound, and the body of the dragon is ignobly tossed into the sea.

The nameless fire-breathing dragon is one of the most common figures in Germanic mythology. Many critics of *Beowulf* believe that the poet added the hero's fight with the dragon in order to give Beowulf a suitably heroic death. Such a valiant hero could not, of course, die peacefully in his bed. Instead, he must die fighting a most terrifying adversary, and

Dragons were common figures in Germanic mythology. The dragon of Beowulf serves as a deadly final adversary for the hero of the story.

such a worthy adversary could not be found among ordinary humans—only in the figure of a dragon.

To the people of the early Middle Ages, dragons were real, although unseen. They believed that buried treasure and gold must lie hidden within the mysterious mounds that dotted the countryside (which were actually tombs raised by much earlier peoples). In their imaginations and their stories, they saw awful supernatural spirits and dragons as the guardians of that treasure.

Grendel

Grendel is the terrifying monster who wreaks havoc and destruction among the Danes before being confronted by the hero Beowulf. Descended from the biblical figure of Cain, who slew his brother, Abel, Grendel represents pure evil. He is a member of the race of outcasts cursed by God and who roam the earth wreaking destruction on right-living people, such as the Danes of Heorot. No ordinary sword made by humans can wound the supernatural Grendel, and Hrothgar, the king of the Danes, is powerless to stop Grendel's assaults.

After his first attack on Heorot, Grendel has thirty Danish knights for lunch. Not satisfied with his bloody feast, he returns year after year; for twelve winters Heorot stands empty and desolate, with the people living in fear. The reign of terror ends one night when Grendel bursts into the hall only to be confronted by the mighty Beowulf, who has posted himself as watchman over the hall. Believing that he has only encountered another Danish knight, Grendel seizes Beowulf but is seized in turn by the hero, who grapples with the monster and tears his arm off. Grendel flees to his lair, where he dies. Beowulf then hangs Grendel's bloody arm and hand in the hall of Heorot as a commemoration of his victory.

Historians and critics have long argued over the meaning of the name *Grendel*. Some believe it is connected with the word *grindan* ("grind") because the monster grinds the flesh and bones of his unhappy captives. Others link *Grendel* with *grund*, a word meaning the bottom of a lake or pool, where the cursed family of monsters dwells alongside its treasure. In this way, *Grendel* can be understood as a name meaning "Water Monster" or "Lake Monster." The trolls and monsters of old Scandinavia were said to dwell in the murky depths of inland waters, where humans feared to go.

For the poet of *Beowulf*, the figure of Grendel represents a darker, uncivilized time, when humans lived by pure strength and cunning alone. Grendel attacks Heorot out of nothing more than jealousy. He cannot stand the thought of humans enjoying themselves by feasting, drinking, and story-telling in the warm hall of Heorot. Grendel prevails for many years but is finally defeated by the forces of reason and civilization, embodied in Beowulf.

Grendel's Mother

Like Grendel, Grendel's mother also belongs to the company of Cain, the race of monsters and demons exiled from Earth by God. She vows revenge for the death of her son at the hands of Beowulf. Although she is a powerful being in her own right, she realizes that she does not have the strength to match Beowulf's. Instead, she tries to defeat the hero by stealth.

> Grendel's mother,
> a monster woman, kept war-grief
> deep in her mind, dwelt in terrible waters,
> icy cold streams, since Cain raised the sword
> against closest kinsman, put blade to his brother.[22]

One night Grendel's mother sneaks into Heorot and captures Aeschere, Hrothgar's favorite knight. She carries him off to her lair, the haunted mere, a frightening landscape of rocks, cliffs, and a high waterfall. Hrothgar then asks for Beowulf's help against the she-monster, and Beowulf accepts the challenge. He sets off for the mere, where he is captured by Grendel's mother and brought down to her dwelling place. Again, Beowulf fights with his hands and is thrown to the ground by the monster. When he spies a sword made by the race of giants, he seizes it, realizing that—unlike man-made swords—this one can wound Grendel's mother. Beowulf slays her with the sword and then cuts off Grendel's head to bring back to Heorot.

Beowulf's battle with Grendel's mother symbolizes the struggle against the chaotic forces of nature, which, in medieval times, posed a constant threat to the well-being of humans. In the poet's time, nature was not inspiring but

61

dangerous, and one risked one's life when venturing alone into forests or mountains. As Beowulf approaches the lair, the poet describes the terrible landscape:

> With a few wise counselors the king rode ahead
> to search out the way, till suddenly he came
> upon stunted firs, gnarled mountain pines
> leaning over stones, cold and gray,
> a joyless wood.[23]

Grendel and his mother are water demons, members of the tribe of mythical half-human, half-animal creatures that menaced ordinary people in the legends of pagan Scandinavia. The defeat of these monsters represents the triumph of humans over the natural world, and the defeat of the old gods by Christianity.

Heardred

The son of Hygelac, Heardred becomes king of the Geats after his father is killed during a raid on the Frisians. Heardred is counseled by the wise Beowulf, who honorably agrees to allow the younger man to become king despite Beowulf's much higher prestige among the Geats. (Heardred's own mother, Queen Hygd, does not believe in her son's ability to rule wisely or well over the Geats.)

Lacking the diplomatic skill of Beowulf, Heardred unwisely becomes involved in the intrigues of the Swedish royal court. He receives the sons of Ohthere, Swedish rebels who rise up against their uncle, King Onela. As a result of his hospitality, Heardred is killed in a duel with Onela, who invades the land of the Geats to pursue his enemies. After Heardred's death, Beowulf ascends the throne and becomes king of the Geats.

The figure of Heardred highlights the much greater ability of Beowulf, both as a fighter and as a king. Whereas Beowulf will rule skillfully over the Geats for fifty years, Heardred's reign is very brief, ending with his unwise meddling in the feuds of a foreign court. And whereas Beowulf wins two difficult combats with supernatural monsters and will later slay a third dragon, Heardred dies ignobly in his first important battle. With the figure of Heardred, the poet of *Beowulf* comments that natural ability is more important than high birth.

Hrothgar

Hrothgar is the king of the Danes, the son of Halfdane, and a member of the dynasty founded by Scyld Scefing. Hrothgar's magnificent royal mead hall, known as Heorot, serves him as a residence, meeting place, and symbol of his authority. Nevertheless, Hrothgar finds himself helpless against the monster Grendel, whose ravages are reported by poets and singers to the Geats.

When Beowulf hears the sad story, he comes to Hrothgar's court. The king allows Beowulf into his presence, and when he hears of Beowulf's promise to come to the aid of the Danes, Hrothgar gladly accepts, promising a just reward in compensation should Beowulf succeed. Hrothgar recalls the time when he gave shelter to Beowulf's father, Ecgtheow, and settled a feud by sending a peace offering of treasure to Ecgtheow's enemies. In return, Ecgtheow gave Hrothgar his loyalty and served the king well.

Hrothgar turns over the watch of Heorot to Beowulf—the first time he has allowed any other man to usurp his authority in the hall. Beowulf's triumph over Grendel does not reflect badly on Hrothgar; he is known far and wide as a good king, one who displays one of the most important traits of a worthy king: generosity. He sings Beowulf's praises after the battle with Grendel, adopts the prince as his son, and offers the Geats a rich reward:

> Then Healfdane's [Halfdane] sword-son gave to Beowulf
> a golden war-standard, ensign of victory

The royal mead hall depicted in this French tapestry provides a glimpse into the setting of Heorot, the hall of the Danish king Hrothgar in Beowulf.

with plated ornament, helmet and mail-shirt,
a jewel-encrusted long-sword, and many saw these
laid before the man.[24]

Hrothgar represents royal authority and just rule. Yet his life also reflects the merciless wheel of fortune, the fact that a time of peace and contentment will inevitably be followed by a time of sorrow, anger, and helplessness. In Hrothgar, the audience witnesses the passing of a former age and an older generation yielding to the greater strength of its sons and descendants.

Hygd

Hygd, Hygelac's queen, appears late in the poem, after Beowulf returns from his mission to the Danes. Like Wealhtheow, Hygd's role is to support her king, and she does it well, behaving generously to the knights and guests in her royal hall. The poet highlights the goodness of Hygd by telling the tale of the very bad queen Modthryth, who would torture and execute any knight who dared to look at her directly.

When King Hygelac dies, Hygd briefly takes center stage in *Beowulf.* Although her son Heardred is next in line for the throne, she has no confidence in his ability and instead supports Beowulf as the next king of the Geats. Among the pagan Germanic tribes, kingship was not necessarily heredi-tary—instead, the worthiest man was elected and raised to the throne by his peers. Hygd's actions reflect this older cus-tom, and the fact that Beowulf allows Heardred to ascend reflects Beowulf's own high sense of honor in submitting to the younger man. (Beowulf also wisely realizes that his taking the throne would probably lead to civil war among the Geats.) The result of this well-intentioned action, however, is strife for the Geats and an early death for Heardred, who does not have the sense to stay out of a civil war among the rival Swedes, and he pays for it with his life.

Hygelac

The king of the Geats, Hygelac is the son of Hrethel and the uncle of Beowulf. He freely gives his permission to Beowulf to sail for Denmark to help Hrothgar, and when Beowulf returns triumphant, Hygelac receives him with a speech of praise. Beowulf turns over to Hygelac, and to his queen, Hygd, a por-tion of the treasure granted to the Geats by Hrothgar. Hygelac returns the favor by granting Beowulf a precious sword, a great expanse of land, and a hall and throne of his own.

This character is based on a historical king named Hygelac, who was known for a failed raid he made against the Frisians in about the year 515. The sixth-century historian Gregory of Tours described this raid in his book *History of the Franks*. In this account, the king comes ashore to attack the land of the Franks but is defeated and slain by Theudebert, the son of the Frankish king Theuderic. Although to Gregory of Tours and the Franks the real Hygelac was nothing more than a pirate, to the author of *Beowulf* he was an upstanding king and a hero.

As a character in the poem, Hygelac does not receive the same attention and detailed description as his nephew, or even of Hrothgar, king of the Danes. But as a just and wor-thy king, he serves to highlight Beowulf's sense of duty and loyalty. He is also the recipient of Beowulf's generous gifts, in the form of treasure from Hrothgar's court. Hygelac's death is told in *Beowulf* as the prelude to Beowulf's own reign over the Geats.

Scyld Scefing

The founder of the dynasty known as the Scyldings, Scyld ("Shield") Scefing appears in the opening lines of *Beowulf*. He was a foundling, a baby cast adrift in a boat. When the Danes, forlorn and without a king, discovered the child on their shores, they adopted him as their new leader. The first hero of *Beowulf* is Scyld Scefing, as the poet describes him:

> Often Scyld Scefing seized mead-benches
> from enemy troops, from many a clan;
> he terrified warriors, even though first he was found
> a waif, helpless. For that came a remedy,
> he grew under heaven, prospered in honors
> until every last one of the bordering nations
> beyond the whale-road had to heed him,
> pay him tribute. He was a good king![25]

Scyld died while still in the prime of his life, but he had prepared for his death with detailed instructions for his funeral. With the description of Scyld's funeral, the poet of *Beowulf* comments that every man knew that death could come at any time, and it was best to be fully prepared.

The Scyldings obediently carried out Scyld's instructions, sending him off in a magnificent prow, laying the king's body out by the mast, and loading the boat with the treasures Scyld had won during his far-flung adventures: fine weapons, battle gear, coats of chain mail, and a gold standard. The Scyldings cast the boat adrift, and the winds and tides carry Scyld out to sea.

With the story of Scyld Scefing and the funeral that begins the story of *Beowulf*, the poet means to set the scene and capture the attention of his audience. This will be no ordinary

The Viking funeral ship that carries the fallen hero Scyld Scefing was similar to this Viking ship dated 850 A.D., found intact in Norway.

story; there will be battles and heroism, treasures found and lost, and finally a death and funeral rites worthy of a great king. Scyld's story is *Beowulf* in miniature, and the deeds and life of Beowulf will echo those of the founder of the Scyldings.

Unferth

A thane in Hrothgar's court, the envious Unferth challenges Beowulf's courage after the Geat arrives in Heorot. Unferth recalls a swimming contest between Beowulf and Breca and the fact that Breca, after seven nights in the storm-tossed waves, arrived first at their destination. Using this story as an example, Unferth predicts that Grendel will also defeat Beowulf.

Beowulf replies with his own version of the contest with Breca. The two men had been friends since childhood and had often dared each other to dangerous tests of their stamina and courage. Instead of a contest, they had taken up a dangerous challenge together, one in which Beowulf himself slew nine sea beasts. By contrast, Beowulf points out, Unferth has carried out no such worthy deeds. Instead, he is known only for killing his own kinsman during a feud, for which he will suffer damnation and a life in Hell after his death.

Unferth has no reply to Beowulf's retort and falls silent. Later in the poem, when Beowulf makes ready to fight Grendel's mother, Unferth offers Beowulf the use of his sword Hrunting, a mighty iron blade forged in the blood of those it had slain and which had never failed any man who wielded it in battle. In exchange, Beowulf declares that if he should die, he would bequeath his own sword to Unferth. Nevertheless, the poet comments that by lending his sword to Beowulf, Unferth again loses standing since he appears unwilling to face the monster himself.

Unferth enjoys high standing in the hall of Heorot and sits next to King Hrothgar. Yet despite his high position and good reputation, he cannot manage to bring Beowulf down to his own level. The figure of Unferth serves to highlight Beowulf's virtues and the fact that not even the best of the Danes comes close to matching them.

Wealhtheow

The queen of Hrothgar, Wealhtheow displays all the queenly virtues: a sense of hospitality, generosity, and modesty. When the Geats arrive at Hrothgar's court, Wealhtheow sees to it that they are properly received, offers the cup first to Hrothgar and then to the guests, and welcomes Beowulf by thanking him for coming and answering her prayers for deliverance from Grendel.

After the fight with Grendel, Wealhtheow warmly receives Beowulf and the Geats back into Heorot. She distributes sumptuous gifts to the deliverers, praises Hrothgar's decision to adopt Beowulf as his son, and then entreats Beowulf to counsel her own two sons, Hrethric and Hrothmund, as they grow into adults and take on their responsibilities.

Beowulf is a poem about heroes and about the deeds of men. The place of women, as shown in the figures of Wealhtheow and Hygd, the queen of Hygelac, is to support their men in every way possible. Wealhtheow represents what was expected of a queen: generosity and an important role as peacemaker. She entreats Beowulf to help her two sons and wishes to avoid any strife among the Danes over the succession

A fourteenth-century painting depicts three allegorical figures representing Charity, Temperance, and Justice. Wealhtheow, one of the few female characters in Beowulf, *embodies these qualities.*

to the throne. But she also appears as a prophet, predicting the future troubles awaiting her sons and her people. In the Germanic world, women were believed to have the gift of foreknowledge, and this belief is reflected in the words of Wealhtheow.

Wiglaf

A Scylding warrior, a son of Weohstan, and a cousin of Beowulf, Wiglaf proves the most courageous of Beowulf's companions when he helps the king in his last, fatal battle with the dragon. When the other knights flee at the dragon's terrifying flame, Wiglaf stands firm, even though it is his first time in combat. Wiglaf reproaches the cowardly behavior of the others. He offers Beowulf the use of his wooden shield, and when the shield is consumed by the dragon's fire, he takes shelter with Beowulf behind an iron shield.

When the dragon then attacks Beowulf, Wiglaf strikes out and inflicts a mortal wound on the dragon, whose flame begins to weaken. In his last moments, Beowulf entreats Wiglaf to bring the dragon's treasure hoard before him so he can look on it before dying. Wiglaf then hears Beowulf's final instructions for his funeral and for the raising of a treasure mound on the Whale's Ness, a cliff that rises from the sea. Beowulf rewards Wiglaf with his golden collar, helmet, and corselet. For his cousin's loyalty, Beowulf—who has no son of his own—will designate Wiglaf as his successor as king of the Geats.

After the death of Beowulf, Wiglaf recounts the battle to Beowulf's unworthy companions. He rebukes them for ingratitude, recalling that Beowulf had generously showered gifts on them in the past. Wiglaf knows that the Geats are doomed—their own cowardice will tempt their enemies to attack them:

Now all treasure, giving and receiving,
all home-joys, ownership, comfort,
shall cease for your kin; deprived of their rights

each man of your families will have to be exiled,
once nobles afar hear of your flight,
a deed of no glory. Death is better
for any warrior than a shameful life![26]

Wiglaf returns to the dragon's hoard and, at the head of seven men, loads the treasure on a cart and brings it to Beowulf's resting place on the Whale's Ness. Wiglaf's actions represent those of an ideal war companion. Among the Germanic peoples, the members of a *comitatus*, or war company, were expected to stand by their leader through thick and thin and to give up their own lives if necessary to protect their lord in battle. To return alive after the defeat or death of their chieftain was considered the ultimate disgrace, an action that would strip them of all rank, possessions, and honor. Wiglaf is the only one of Beowulf's companions to rise to the occasion and face the dragon's fire, and for this he is appropriately rewarded by Beowulf just before the king's death.

CHAPTER FIVE

Themes in *Beowulf*

Critics of *Beowulf* have pointed out that this ancient poem is a close relative of the myth of the "Bear's Son," a folktale that has been recounted in many different forms and times throughout the world. In this myth, a young hero is raised in the wild by bears—in some cases, wolves—and lives far from human society. When he reaches adulthood, the hero becomes a leader of men who clashes with dragons and demons. He performs many feats of strength and daring, including the rescue of a princess from a monster's underground lair. The setting of the story changes, as do many other details, but its main themes of glory seeking and heroism lie at the heart of the *Beowulf* story.

The poet of *Beowulf* sets his tale among rocky cliffs, dark forests, and waterfalls, a landscape imagined by the Anglo-Saxons as the homeland of their ancestors. The hero is a prince of the Geats, a vanished Germanic tribe whose ultimate fate lay shrouded in mystery, even for medieval Englishmen. The poet describes Beowulf's clash with the demons as an act of pure glory-seeking heroism, in which he rescues the court of the Danish king from a terrible destruction. In the finale, *Beowulf's* hero dies, an event that dooms the Geats to conquest by outsiders.

Beowulf is a tale of past glories, but many of its principal themes reflect the concerns of its original audience. The men and women who first heard *Beowulf* were emerging from an illiterate pagan past and adapting themselves to a new religion and a new kind of society. Many historians have found in *Beowulf* a description of the struggle and bloodshed that occurs when newcomers impose new "civilization" on a people who live by older traditions. In the Anglo-Saxon migrations and the period of early Christianity, states author James W. Earl,

> we have the makings of a heroic age not unlike that on the American frontier during the westward expansion, characterized by military organization, war with the native inhabitants, large land claims, power struggles, masculine violence, exploitation, and lawlessness. This state of affairs would have been modified gradually by traditional forms of law and order, the slow reemergence of women, stable kinship structures, and settled agricultural communities. This period...is what we find reflected in narratives of the Heroic Age like *Beowulf.* Beowulf depicts a struggle to impose order on real social chaos.[27]

A twelfth-century illustration portrays a clash between knights and peasants. Anglo-Saxon society was extremely violent, and Beowulf *is, in part, the story of a struggle to impose order on social chaos.*

The difficult transition between these two worlds brings much of the tension of the story, in which the old virtues of courage, loyalty, faithful service, and gift giving clash with Christian piety, humility, charity, and faith in the hereafter. The *Beowulf* poet looks back on the past, regretting the old battles but in the end setting this past to rest for a nostalgic audience. In the words of Earl, "Heroic poetry generally does serve to prolong a culture's identification with a lost past while at the same time acknowledging that past as irretrievably lost. As an act of mourning, it fixes an image of what has been lost...until the object is internalized, and the loss is accepted and carried forward into the new possibilities that it has opened for the future."[28]

Civilization and Nature

In *Beowulf*, as in all medieval literature, the natural world represents not beauty or poetic inspiration but rather a dangerous, chaotic, and menacing force. For the Germanic tribes of northern Europe, the forests held wild beasts and supernatural monsters, and the awful storms of summer and the bitter frosts of winter posed mortal threats. Only a very unwise person would venture into the forest, or upon the open sea, alone. To meet nature on even terms, humans had to build ships, weapons, and fortified halls, which symbolized their mastery over their surroundings.

To allay their great fears of nature, medieval people lived closely huddled in walled towns and sheltered villages. They traveled only a few well-trod paths from one place to the next, only in daylight and always in company. The Germanic pagans made ritual human and animal sacrifices to natural spirits of the weather and of the seasons, hoping to propitiate the gods who might otherwise unleash a deadly wrath.

The story and setting of *Beowulf* reflects this primal fear of nature. Nature does not represent an escape or solace, as it did for many poets and authors of a much later time. According to critic Fred C. Robinson,

Men in that day found no more comfort in nature per se than a thoughtful modern man finds in typhoons, black holes, or atomic fission today. Nature seemed anarchic, inimical, and life was endurable only in so far as man had imposed rational order upon it. The vernal woods were menacing, beset with fens and wolf-slopes, fires and storms, and uncontrolled monstrous life.[29]

In *Beowulf*, nature is represented most vividly by the demon Grendel and his mother, who live in haunted swamps and terrifying black pools. Nature, as the poet represents it, has always been the place for Cain's race of monsters:

> They are fatherless creatures,
> and their whole ancestry is hidden in a past
> of demons and ghosts. They dwell apart
> among wolves on the hills, on windswept crags
> and treacherous keshes [marshes], where cold streams
> pour down the mountain and disappear
> under mist and moorland.[30]

An engraving illustrates mythical sea monsters. The story of Beowulf *plays with contemporary misconceptions of nature to create drama and danger.*

Nature is chaos, a fearsome place that kills. It can only be conquered by the weapons, armor, and tools of humans. This conquest was the task of civilization, which put a human design on chaotic nature in the form of plowed fields, cleared forests, walled villages and towns, and castles raised on prominent hilltops. Within these artificial structures, humans took pleasure in each other's company, in feasting, drinking, storytelling, and other amusements. The joyous feasting within the hall of Heorot symbolizes civilization, and for that reason the hall enrages Grendel, the symbol of the evil natural world.

The monster and its actions represent the opposite of the ceremonies and careful ritual of King Hrothgar's court. For his audience, the poet of *Beowulf* evokes the struggle of humans against nature and the endless campaign to subdue the many dangers found just outside one's home or village. By braving a journey to the monster's lair, and by the strength of his hands, Beowulf defeats the natural world and ends Grendel's uncontrolled ravagings among the Danes. The fact that he fights alone makes Beowulf's actions all the more heroic, for pagan society dictated that no man could thrive outside the system of mutual obligation and personal loyalty.

Loyalty and Gift Giving

Vital aspects of the past for the original audience of *Beowulf* were the giving of gifts and personal loyalty. There were no nations to which one might pledge allegiance or feel the sentiment of patriotism. Instead, loyalty and obedience were owed to an individual.

The men who make up the court of Hrothgar live by this code, which formed the foundation of pagan society. Each man belongs to a war company—in Germanic society, a *comitatus*—and serves his chieftain, a leader chosen for his bravery and charisma. This bond confers obligations on both sides. The follower, or thane, must always stand ready to fight—and if necessary give up his life—on behalf of the chief. If he fails in his duty, and leaves the field of battle alive after a defeat or the death of his leader, he suffers disgrace and ostracism. To have no *comitatus* is the worst event that can befall a pagan warrior. If he suffers this fate, he must live alone and without protection and must fend for himself in the hostile, deadly natural world.

Because no human can survive alone, the heroes and knights of *Beowulf* depend on one another, as the nineteenth-century English historian John Earle points out:

> *Mutual dependence is the law of human society.* No one is independent; not the strongest or the noblest or most exalted; for he depends upon the support of those who are under him. Consideration and generosity from him to them; honour and fidelity and devotion from them to him; these are the rudimentary foundations upon which alone it is possible to erect and edify a stable fabric of government, to build up a State.[31]

These relationships arose from a society constantly prepared for war and for honorable death in battle. For that reason, the cold-blooded murder of a loyal thane, Aeschere, by Grendel's mother is an event that breaks the customary bonds and brings deep anguish to King Hrothgar:

> Now this powerful
> other one arrives, this force for evil
> driven to avenge her kinsman's death.
> Or so it seems to thanes in their grief,
> in the anguish every thane endures
> at the loss of a ring-giver, now that the hand
> that bestowed so richly has been stilled in death.[32]

The leader returns this loyalty with the giving of gifts—treasure, weapons, horses, slaves, women—won in battle or during a raid on an enemy town or camp. Presenting the valuable armor and sword to Beowulf after Beowulf's tri-

Gift giving, a theme of Beowulf, *often centers on the spoils of war. Armor, such as this seventh-century Viking helmet, was a valuable gift.*

umph over Grendel makes Hrothgar, in the eyes of the poet, a noble and worthy king. Gift giving is also an important part of diplomacy; when one king wishes to ally himself with another, he must send a gift to his potential friend. These gifts represent not only generosity but also wealth and power. A chieftain who skimps on gift giving not only may lose the loyalty of his followers but also the friendship of neighbors, who always stand ready to attack kings they see as weaker and less worthy of respect.

When the system of loyalty and gift giving is broken or violated in some way, the consequences can be dire. In *Beowulf*, the thief who simply steals a golden cup from the treasure hoard of a dragon risks bringing the monster's righteous wrath down on his entire nation. In his final and fatal fight with the dragon, Beowulf pays for this low crime with his life and gains no advantage for the unworthy Geats, who can claim no part of the cursed treasure hoard.

The Virtue of Vengeance

In the pagan Germanic world, humility and sacrifice were not celebrated. Instead, the Germanic people valued courage in battle, loyalty to their kin and their chieftains, and the righting of wrongs by personal vengeance. The taking of vengeance was a matter of honor and necessity in the Germanic world, where there was no written law code to live by or courts to judge disputes between tribes or individuals. Instead, the taking of life was to be redeemed by vengeance or by the payment of blood money, also known as wergild, by the killer. Vengeance was a matter of sacred honor, as pointed out by William Witherle Lawrence: "If the king or any member of the comitatus were slain or injured, the duty of vengeance fell upon the rest of the band. Similarly, revenge for injuries inflicted upon any member of the family or clan group was a sacred obligation resting upon all other members; until the injury had been wiped out, the honor of the clan was darkly tarnished."[33]

The spirit of revenge led to feuds lasting generations. Aggrieved relatives or a king's retainers might seize their opportunity to strike at their rivals with even greater violence. The revenge for this action, in turn, could lead to a spiral of bloody feuding. But the poet of *Beowulf* understands the virtue of vengeance, describing it as an irresistible urge for the wronged leader Hengest in the "Finnsburg" episode:

Then winter was gone,
earth's lap grew lovely,
longing woke
in the cooped-up exile
for a voyage home—
but more for vengeance,
some way of bringing
things to a head:
his sword arm hankered
to greet the Jutes.[34]

Likewise, the mother of Grendel seeks vengeance for the death of her son, and Hrothgar seeks his vengenace for the monster's killing of his favorite thane. But when Ecgtheow flees to the court of Hrothgar after committing a killing among the Geats, Hrothgar settles the matter by sending money back to the injured clan. This peaceable righting of a wrong bound Ecgtheow to Hrothgar's service. Hrothgar recalls this generous act when he first meets Ecgtheow's son, Beowulf.

The ideal of vengeance creates tension between the pagan and Christian worlds. Personal vengeance, and feuding for the sake of honor, had no place in the new religion. When wronged, Christians were expected to turn the other cheek and to fight the sin of pride. In the opinion of critic Dorothy Whitelock, the poet and the audience of *Beowulf* were thoroughly Christian—but they were Christians who still accepted the virtue of vengeance:

> [Any] man of the audience might find himself suddenly forced to become an avenger by necessity, perhaps in circumstances that involved his acting counter to his inclination and affections. . . . One may reach the conclusion that the audience of *Beowulf* was a Christian company, and one which admitted that vengeance, in unavoidable circumstances and carried out in accordance with the law, was a binding duty.[35]

The Mysterious Workings of Fate

Another vital aspect of the pagan world, the notion of Fate, looms over the actions of Beowulf and other characters in the poem. In the time of Beowulf, this notion was giving way to the Christian idea of right living and the afterlife—punishment in hell for sinners and a heavenly reward for the faithful and virtuous. In the world of Anglo-Saxon heroes and monsters, however, there was no escaping one's destiny, no matter how cruel it might be.

The people of the pagan Germanic world recognized one overpowering, invisible force that controlled human destiny: fate, a thing that no one could escape. Fate was a mysterious force that snared humans in an inescapable web. Their luck might be good or bad—as fate had already determined. Despite one's good intentions, fate had decided the results of one's actions beforehand, and efforts against adversity and death were useless. There was no Heaven and Hell in the Germanic world, and there was no serene paradise awaiting those who lived a sinless life. There was only fate, which was determined before one's birth and which, in the end, brought an inevitable death.

Beowulf, as a pagan hero, stands up to fate. He still does what he believes is right and honorable, even though it will bring his destruction. Essayist Sarah F. McNary describes the poem and Beowulf's attitude as follows:

> Over the whole poem broods the thought of Wyrd [Fate]. The atmosphere is gray and misty, like the marsh home of Grendel, and through the grayness go stalking the huge dim forms of the giants and *nickers* of the northern cult. . . . There is, however, no disposition to sit down and weep over the melancholy of it. Beowulf stands up bravely and looks the issue in the face—Fate must be fought against, whatever the odds.[36]

A sense of death and doom overshadows Beowulf, as the poet several times predicts the death of his main character and the deadly events to come in the final section of the work. Destruction will also overtake Beowulf's nation, the Geats, who must fall to the invading Swedes after the death of their king. For the poet of *Beowulf* and his audience, the rise and fall of nations was a common occurrence, an awesome, calamitous aspect of fate that could not be explained by the earthly actions of kings, knights, and armies. The *Beowulf* poet lived among the ruins of Roman Britain, the northernmost outpost of a once-powerful empire. His audience had heard many tales of the destruction of the Celtic Britons by the Anglo-Saxons, and they lived in a time when the petty kingdoms of the Anglo-Saxons were engaged in constant warfare.

This sense of ultimate failure and destruction was a central tenet of fate and of the old religion, which predicted the end of the world in a cataclysmic battle known as Ragnarok. But at the time of *Beowulf's* writing, the workings of "Wyrd" were falling away and the promises of Heaven and Hell were arriving in the words of the Bible and the sermons and promises of Christian missionaries.

The Conflict of Two Worlds

The poet of *Beowulf* lived at a time when two worldviews were still in close conflict. The old paganism was dying out, and the new faith of Christianity was arriving from two directions: from the continent of Europe, where the church of Rome and its strict hierarchy had replaced the institutions of the old pagan empire, and from Ireland, where devout missionaries under the banner of St. Patrick came to convert the pagans of northern Britain.

Poetry and literature did not escape this conflict of past and present. Although the Anglo-Saxons of England knew and often heard the old tales of the pagan past, many of the leaders of the new religion considered this sacrilegious and not worthy of a proper Christian. The leaders of the church greatly feared the return of the people, nostalgic for a better and more heroic past, to their old gods.

Christian priests, bishops, and monastery abbots knew that many Christians, in their leisure time, enjoyed the tales of old. In a letter to the monks of the Lindisfarne monastery in northern England, the scholar Alcuin makes the following stern reprimand:

> Let the word of God be read at the meal of the clergy. There it is proper to hear a reader, not a harp-player; to hear sermons of the church fathers, not songs of the laity. What has [the pagan Heathobard king] Ingeld to do with Christ? The house is narrow; it cannot hold both. The King of Heaven will have nothing to do with so-called kings who are heathen and damned, for

that King reigns in Heaven eternally, while the heathen one is damned and laments in Hell.[37]

Christianity was a radical departure from the old beliefs in courage, personal loyalty to earthly lords, the taking of vengeance as a matter of honor, and the giving of gifts and distribution of loot for valor in bloody combat. The transformation reached every level of society and affected nearly every aspect of daily life. It took many decades for the new religion to take hold, and when it finally did, its believers still had many centuries to completely escape the habits and beliefs of paganism. *Beowulf* represents an important landmark on that long and winding path, a very rare work of secular literature that directly reflects the religious conflict and controversies of its day.

In the final lines of the poem, the old religion is symbolically buried, in the form of the dragon's useless hoard, with Beowulf:

They buried torques in the barrow, and jewels
and a trove of such things as trespassing men
had once dared to drag from the hoard.
They let the ground keep that ancestral treasure,
as useless to men now as it ever was.[38]

Many critics of *Beowulf* have seen this religious transformation as an important, deliberate theme of the poet. This individual was witnessing the decline and disappearance of the old Germanic religion, which recognized not a single, omnipotent god in Heaven but a pantheon of Nordic gods such as Odin, Thor, Baldur, and Freya, who originated in Earth spirits worshiped in prehistoric times. According to the old beliefs, on their deaths the heroes on Earth were escorted by the Valkyries to Valhalla, a great drinking hall where they spent their time feasting, drinking, and recounting their heroic exploits while they lived on Earth.

The new religion brought an entirely new outlook on life. The missionaries who arrived in Britain from Ireland and from the continent of Europe told of the one true god, who made the world in six days and rested on the seventh, and whose son, Jesus, walked on Earth and suffered crucifixion for his beliefs. The humility and sacrifice of Jesus were to be emulated by all Christian believers, who were told to love their brothers, help the poor and the sick, and give up their worldly belongings.

A Virtuous Hero

Christianity meant not only a new monotheism but also a drastic change in culture and society. Solitary heroes—such as those exemplified by Beowulf—were passing out of style. According to critic Maurice B. McNamee, Beowulf himself shows this by actions that are motivated not just by the quest for glory but also by charity toward others:

> As we have seen, Beowulf was certainly not unaffected by the motive of personal honor, but it was to be won through the generous service of others. The chief motive for his actions in all three of the major episodes of the poem is the succor and welfare of others—of those who were not even his own countrymen in the first two episodes, and of his own subjects in the third episode. . . . The poet leaves us with no possible room for doubt that charity is a prominent motive in the poem.[39]

By the eighth century the Anglo-Saxon kings had accepted Christianity and had allied themselves with the organized church, with its priests, bishops, missions, monasteries, and earthly leader, the pope. These kings still lived by a code of honor, and they still valued courage in battle. The harsh and violent conditions of the day demanded they turn a blind eye to the suffering and death of others. But to some extent, the Christian virtues of charity, modesty, and piety were replacing the old ideals of courage in battle and loyalty to an earthly chieftain. To symbolize and demonize the gods and beliefs of the past, the *Beowulf* poet used his monsters, especially

An early Christian mosaic of Christ enthroned. The character of Beowulf exemplifies a number of Christian virtues.

Grendel, who kills out of jealousy and who is imagined as descended from Cain, who is cursed by the Christian god for the murder of his own brother.

While the poet made his characters pagan, he described their actions with a firmly held Christian belief, in which a nameless and omnipotent god had created the world. At the end of the poem, Beowulf thinks back on his life, reviewing his pagan and Christian virtues in preparation for death:

I took what came,
cared for and stood by things in my keeping,
never fomented quarrels, never
swore to a lie. All this consoles me,
doomed as I am and sickening for death;

An engraving of King Arthur and the Lady of the Lake. Many tales, such as King Arthur, utilized the Christian virtues exemplified in Beowulf.

because of my right ways, the Ruler of mankind
need never blame me when the breath leaves my body
for murder of kinsman.[40]

The poem ends with lines on the good Christian qualities that all princes should have—qualities personified in the figure of the pagan hero and king Beowulf. In this way the *Beowulf* poet is not just a storyteller but also a teacher, illustrating the new faith to an audience that still held a collective memory of the heroes and legends of the old.

In his essay "*Beowulf*," critic Charles W. Kennedy describes the transformation of paganism into Christianity in the poem:

> Certain it is that under the pen of the *Beowulf* poet the stubborn stuff of Scandinavian legend is tempered and refined, and there emerges the figure of a noble and Christian king. The poem reflects the spirit, not of Scandinavia, but of English life of the seventh and eighth centuries, presenting a blending of old folkways with new, a welding of pagan heroism with Christian virtue.[41]

Beowulf also illustrates the dawning of an age in which raw courage and heroism are giving way to the temper of nobility and the spirit of magnanimity. Prince Beowulf in his youth seeks only the glory of triumph over a terrible enemy; as an aged king, he sacrifices himself singlehandedly for the sake of a thief and for his unworthy followers.

Even though his efforts to save the Geats must fail, Beowulf still upholds the sense of duty to a nation, which has replaced the old pagan virtue of personal loyalty to a chieftain. The authors who will follow the poet of *Beowulf* will devote their works to these new Christian virtues, which will develop into the code of knightly chivalry. They will look back on the long-dead heroes, such as King Arthur, and envelop them in this new code of honor. In *Beowulf*, the reader sees the pagan kings and heroes as they really lived and understands a mysterious and tumultuous society firsthand.

Notes

Introduction: The Strange and Eloquent Music of *Beowulf*

1. Seamus Heaney, trans., *Beowulf: A New Verse Translation.* New York: Farrar, Straus & Giroux, 2000, p. ix.

2. Dennis Poupard and Jelena O. Krstovic, eds., *Classical and Medieval Literature Criticism, vol. 1.* Detroit: Gale Research, 1988, p. 53.

Chapter 1: A Mysterious Author, a Mysterious Time

3. Dorothy Whitelock, "The Audience of *Beowulf.*" Oxford, UK: Clarendon, 1951, pp. 24–25.

4. Quoted in Colin Chase, ed., "The Dating of *Beowulf.*" Toronto, Canada: University of Toronto Press, 1997, p. 20.

5. W.J. Courthope, *A History of English Poetry: The Middle Ages, vol. 1.* London: MacMillan, 1919, p. 79.

6. Quoted in Donald K. Fry, ed., *The "Beowulf" Poet: A Collection of Critical Essays.* Englewood Cliffs, NJ: Prentice-Hall, 1968, pp. 36–37.

7. Quoted in Fry, *The "Beowulf" Poet*, pp. 85–86.

8. William Witherle Lawrence, *"Beowulf" and Epic Tradition.* New York: Hafner, 1961, p. 280.

9. D.H. Crawford, trans., *Beowulf.* New York: Cooper Square, 1966, lines 107–14.

10. Crawford, *Beowulf*, lines 683–87.

11. Crawford, *Beowulf*, lines 86–98.

12. Margaret E. Goldsmith, *The Mode and Meaning of "Beowulf."* London: Athlone, 1970, p. 10.

Chapter 2: The Historical Background of *Beowulf*

13. James W. Earl, *Thinking About "Beowulf."* Stanford, CA: Stanford University Press, 1994, pp. 102–103.

14. Crawford, *Beowulf*, lines 696–702.

15. Quoted in Jess B. Bessinger Jr. and Robert F. Yeager, eds., *Approaches to Teaching "Beowulf."* New York: Modern Language Association of America, 1984, p. 110.

16. Crawford, *Beowulf*, lines 2355–62.

17. Crawford, *Beowulf*, lines 1179–87.

18. Howell D. Chickering Jr., trans., *Beowulf: A Dual-Language Edition*. Garden City, NY: Anchor Books, 1977, lines 1150–54.

19. Lawrence, *"Beowulf" and Epic Tradition*, pp. 248–49.

20. Sarah F. McNary, "Beowulf and Arthur as English Ideals," *Poet Lore*, vol. 6, no. 11, November 1894, p. 532.

Chapter 4: The Cast of Characters

21. Heaney, *Beowulf*, lines 1177–83.

22. Chickering, *Beowulf*, lines 1258–62.

23. Chickering, *Beowulf*, lines 1412–16.

24. Chickering, *Beowulf*, lines 1020–24.

25. Chickering, *Beowulf*, lines 4–11.

26. Chickering, *Beowulf*, lines 2884–91.

Chapter 5: Themes in *Beowulf*

27. Earl, *Thinking About "Beowulf,"* p. 131.

28. Earl, *Thinking About "Beowulf,"* pp. 37–38.

29. Quoted in Poupard and Krstovic, *Classical and Medieval Literature Criticism*, p. 153.

30. Heaney, *Beowulf*, lines 1355–61.

31. John Earle, *The Deeds of Beowulf: An English Epic of the Eighth Century Done into Modern Prose*. Oxford, UK: Clarendon, 1892, p. ix.

32. Heaney, *Beowulf*, lines 1338–44.

33. Lawrence, *"Beowulf" and Epic Tradition*, p. 55.

34. Heaney, *Beowulf*, lines 1138–41.

35. Whitelock, *The Audience of "Beowulf,"* p. 19.

36. McNary, "Beowulf and Arthur as English Ideals," p. 531.

37. Quoted in Bessinger and Yeager, *Approaches to Teaching "Beowulf,"* p. 116.

38. Heaney, *Beowulf,* lines 3163–68.

39. Maurice B. McNamee, *Honor and the Epic Hero: A Study of the Shifting Concept of Magnanimity in Philosophy and Epic Poetry.* New York: Holt, Rinehart, and Winston, 1960, pp. 100–101.

40. Heaney, *Beowulf,* lines 2736–43.

41. Quoted Charles W. Kennedy, *The Earliest English Poetry: A Critical Survey of the Poetry Written Before the Norman Conquest with Illustrative Translations.* Oxford, UK: Oxford University Press, 1943, p. 97.

For Further Exploration

Below are some suggestions for potential essays on *Beowulf.*

1. Historians and critics have debated the identity of the *Beowulf* author and his religious convictions. Do Christian or pagan messages emerge triumphant at the end of *Beowulf*? *See also* "History of Manuscript" in *Beowulf: A Dual Language Edition.*

2. Is the *Beowulf* manuscript an original work of poetry or a copy of an earlier work? What evidence of the poem and language supports these rival contentions, and which seems to emerge victorious? *See also* Ritchie Girvan, *"Beowulf" and the Seventh Century: Language and Content.* London: Methuen, 1971 pp. 9–11; Kevin S. Kiernan, "The Eleventh-Century Origin of Beowulf and the *Beowulf* Manuscript," in *The Dating of "Beowulf."* Ed. Colin Chase. Toronto, Canada: University of Toronto Press, 1997.

3. The act of giving gifts and rewards follows Beowulf's slaying of Grendel and Grendel's mother. How does the distribution of treasure and loot hold together the society described in *Beowulf*? *See* Simon Schama, *A History of Britain: At the Edge of the World?* 300 B.C.–A.D. 1603. New York: Hyperion, 2000; John M. Hill, *The Cultural World in "Beowulf."* Toronto, Canada: University of Toronto Press, 1995.

4. Is Beowulf an altruistic hero or a loot-seeking adventurer in his voyage to Denmark and his offer to the Danes to slay the monster Grendel? *See also* Elizabeth M. Liggins, "Revenge and Reward as Recurrent Motives in *Beowulf,*" Neuphilologische Mitteilungen, vol. 74, 1973, pp. 193–13; William Whallon, "Formulas for Heroes in the *Iliad* and in *Beowulf,*" Modern Philology, vol. 63, November, 1965, pp. 95–104; John M. Hill, "The Economy of Honour," in *The Cultural World in "Beowulf."* Toronto, Canada: University of Toronto Press, 1995; Margaret E. Goldsmith, "The Nature of the Hero," in *The Mode and Meaning of "Beowulf."* London: Athlone, 1970.

5. The monsters of *Beowulf* are central to the action of the poem. They are Beowulf's adversaries, but they are much more than that: They are symbols of forces opposing civilization as well as Christianity. How does the *Beowulf* poet emphasize the danger, terror, and otherworldliness of Grendel, Grendel's mother, and

the dragon? *See also* J.R.R. Tolkien, "The Monsters and the Critics," *The "Beowulf" Poet: A Collection of Critical Essays.* Ed. Donald K. Fry. Englewood Cliffs, NJ: Prentice-Hall, 1968, pp. 21–32; William Witherle Lawrence, "Grendel and His Dam" and "The Dragon" in *"Beowulf" and Epic Tradition.* New York: Hafner, 1961; G. Storm, "Grendel the Terrible," Neuphilologische Mitteilungen, vol. 73, 1972, pp. 427–36.

6. After Beowulf arrives at Heorot, he is challenged by Unferth, one of Hrothgar's thanes. How does the poet use Unferth to highlight the achievements and ability of Beowulf, and how is Unferth's challenge resolved? *See also* Morton W. Bloomfield, "Beowulf and Christian Allegory: An Interpretation of Unferth," in *The "Beowulf" Poet: A Collection of Critical Essays.* Ed. Donald K. Fry. Englewood Cliffs, NJ: Prentice-Hall, 1968, William Witherle Lawrence, "Scyld and Breca" in *"Beowulf" and Epic Tradition.* New York: Hafner, 1961; Edward B. Irving Jr., "Characters and Kings," in *Rereading "Beowulf."* Philadelphia: University of Pennsylvania Press, 1989, pp. 36–47.

7. Many critics and readers of *Beowulf* have seen the hall of Heorot as a symbol and metaphor for advancing civilization, set against the dark forces of the wilderness. How does Heorot represent the human conquest of nature and its dangerous, chaotic aspects? *See also* Edward B. Irving Jr., "The Hall as Image and Character," in *Rereading "Beowulf."* Philadelphia: University of Pennsylvania Press, 1989; James W. Earl, "The Hall and the Hut," in *Thinking About "Beowulf."* Stanford, CA: Stanford University Press, 1994.

8. What is the function of the Finnsburg story, a long "digression" from the main plot of *Beowulf* that many readers find bewildering? Why did the poet place this episode where he did, and what does the episode accomplish for the audience? *See also* Stanley B. Greenfield, "The Finn Episode and Its Parallel," in *A Critical History of Old English Literature*, New York: New York University Press, 1965, pp. 90–91; and Adrien Bonjour, *The Digressions in "Beowulf."* Oxford, UK: Blackwell, 1950.

9. The poet sees Beowulf's death in battle with the treasure-hoarding dragon as an inevitable aspect of his fate—the preordained events that make up the web of everyday life and human action.

In what ways does the poet evoke the notion of tragedy and fate? *See also* Alvin A. Lee, "Symbolic Metaphor and the Design of *Beowulf*," in Joseph Tuso, ed., *Beowulf*. Trans. E. Talbot Donaldson. New York: W.W. Norton, 1975; F. Anne Payne, "Three Aspects of Wyrd in *Beowulf*," in Robert B. Burlin and Edward B. Irving Jr., eds., *Old English Studies in Honour of John C. Pope*; Toronto: Toronto University Press, 1974; and Ursula Dronke, "Beowulf and Ragnarok," *Saga-Book*, vol. 17, 1969–1970, pp. 302–25.

10. *Beowulf* begins and ends with funerals: that of Scyld Scefing, the founder of the Danish Scylding dynasty, to begin the poem, and that of Beowulf himself of the Geats to end it. Compare and contrast the ceremonies and physical settings of these rites. What do these royal funerals represent for the Danes and for the Geats? *See also* Sam Newton, *The Origins of "Beowulf" and the Pre-Viking Kingdom of East Anglia*. Cambridge, U.K: S.A. Brewer, 1994. pp. 43–53.

Appendix of Criticism

Beowulf as a Contemporary Song

The war-ship and the mead-hall bring us back to that early era of society, when great men knew only to be heroes, flattered by their bards, whose songs are ever the echoes of their age and their patrons.... Beowulf may be a god or a nonentity, but the poem which records his exploits must at least be true, true in the manners it paints and the emotions which the poet reveals—the emotions of his contemporaries.

Isaac Disraeli, "Beowulf-the Hero-Life,"
in *Amenities of Literature, Consisting of
Sketches and Characters of English Literature.*
London: Frederick Warne, 1881.

The Valiant and Selfless Hero

Rude as the poetry is, its hero is grand; he is so, simply by his deeds. Faithful, first to his prince, then to his people, he went alone, in a strange land, to venture himself for the delivery of his fellow-men; he forgets himself in death, while thinking only that it profits others.... Compare with him the monsters whom he destroys, the last traditions of the ancient wars against inferior races, and of the primitive religion; think of his life of danger, nights upon the waves, man grappling with the brute creation, man's indomitable will crushing the breasts of beasts; man's powerful muscles which, when exerted, tear the flesh of the monsters; you will see reappear through the mist of legends, and under the light of poetry, the valiant men who, amid the madness of war and the raging of their own mood, began to settle a people and to found a state.

Hippolyte A. Taine, "The Saxons,"
in *History of English Literature. Vol. 1.*
New York: Hurst, n.d.

A Rough-Hewn Epic

One of the oldest and most important remains of Anglo-Saxon literature is the epic poem of *Beowulf*. Its age is unknown, but it comes from a very distant and hoary antiquity; somewhere between the seventh and tenth centuries. It is like a piece of ancient armor; rusty and battered, and yet strong. From within comes a voice sepulchral, as if the ancient armor spoke, telling a simple, straight-forward narrative; with here and there the boastful speech of a rough old Dane, reminding one of those made by the heroes of Homer.

> Henry Wadsworth Longfellow, "Anglo-Saxon Language and Poetry," in *The Poets and Poetry of Europe with Introductions and Biographical Notices.* Boston: Houghton, Mifflin, 1882.

Imagining a Performance of *Beowulf*

Great imagination is not one of the excellences of *Beowulf*, but it has pictorial power of a fine kind, and the myth of summer and winter on which it rests is out of the imagination of the natural and early world. It has a clear vision of places and things and persons; it has preserved for us two monstrous types out of the very early world. When we leave out the repetitions which oral poetry created and excuses, it is rapid and direct; and the dialogue is brief, simple and human. Finally, we must not judge it in the study. If we wish to feel whether *Beowulf* is good poetry, we should place ourselves, as evening draws on, in the hall of the folk, when the benches are filled with warriors, merchants and seamen, and the Chief sits in the high seat, and the fires flame down the midst, and the cup goes round—and hear the Shaper strike the harp to sing this heroic lay.

> Stopford A. Brooke, *"Beowulf" in English Literature: From the Beginning to the Norman Conquest.* New York: Macmillan, 1921.

The Misplaced Focus of the Poem

The fault of *Beowulf* is that there is nothing much in the story. The hero is occupied in killing monsters, like Hercules or Theseus. But there are other things in the lives of Hercules and Theseus besides the killing of the Hydra or of Procrustes. Beowulf has nothing else to do, when he has killed Grendel and Grendel's mother in Denmark . . . the great beauty, the real value of *Beowulf* is in its dignity of style. In construction it is curiously weak, in a sense preposterous; for while the main story is simplicity itself, the merest commonplace of heroic legend, all about it, in the historic allusions, there are revelations of a whole world of tragedy, plots different in import from that of *Beowulf*, more like the tragic themes of Iceland. Yet with this radical defect, a disproportion that puts the irrelevances in the centre and the serious things on the outer edges, the poem of *Beowulf* is unmistakably heroic and weighty.

W.P. Ker, "The Teutonic Language,"
in *The Dark Ages.* New York:
Thomas Nelson and Sons, 1955.

Beowulf's Dim Views of the World

The world is dim in which these Viking heroes have their being. We can discern the glitter of the sea, but when we pass inland from the shore a thick mist descends. Within the mist lurk terrors by night and day. We are conscious of death by sea and land, but of what life may be we have no idea. It seems to hold no joys; there is no light to reveal it. Beowulf himself is only a great shadow in the surrounding gloom. He might be a Patagonian for all we know about him, or indeed for all we care.

J. Middleton Murry, review of *Beowulf*,
Nation and the Athenaem,
vol. 30, no. 4., October 22, 1921.

The Wild Imaginings of the Poet

It is partly historical, and to this it owes its peculiar fascination, because here is something definite, based on the long progress of the race. Here are persons, who, remote as they are, share in some measure our own passions and capacities, but it is embroidered, as it were, with ornament of sheer fabulous invention, which transcends our experience, and is indeed incredible and preposterous. Here are real kings and fighting men, actual ships and familiar landscape, and here are also giants and genii, impossible monsters and feats of physical endurance to which the wildest credulity, it would seem, could never give credence.

Edmund Gosse, *More Books on the Table.*
New York: Charls Scribners Sons, 1921.

Anglo-Saxon Ideals in *Beowulf*

Certain it is that under the pen of the *Beowulf* poet the stubborn stuff of Scandinavian legend is tempered and refined, and there emerges the figure of a noble and Christian king. The poem reflects the spirit, not of Scandinavia, but of English life of the seventh and eighth centuries, presenting a blending of old folkways with new, a welding of pagan heroism with Christian virtue. The miracle of the *Beowulf* is the artistry of its refashioning. However widely the poem may range through the tribal lands of Scandinavia, the mood and spirit are the mood and spirit of England; the poetic ideal is the Christian ideal.

Charles W. Kennedy, *The Earliest English Poetry:*
A Critical Survey of the Poetry Written Before the
Norman Conquest with Illustrative Translations.
Oxford, UK: Oxford University Press, 1943.

Beowulf's Flawed Dignity

Beowulf is no *Iliad*. The story is mere folklore: Beowulf—the bees' foe, the bear—is one of those folktale heroes who have been suckled by a wild beast and imbibed its strength, and his three exploits are too like one another. The story, then, is a poor one, and there is not enough of it: it has to be padded out to 3,000 lines with digressions and long speeches. Yet there are noble things in *Beowulf*—not only loyalty and dauntless courage but courtesy in hall and respect for ladies; the style too has a grave dignity throughout; and the figure of the old king going out to fight and, as he knows, to die for his people, is truly heroic.

Herbert J.C. Grierson and J.C. Smith, "Anglo-Saxon Poetry,"
in *A Critical History of English Poetry.*
London: Chatto & Windus, 1965.

The Poem's Undeniable Power

A comparison of *Beowulf* with the superb Homeric poems is naturally highly disadvantageous to the Old English epic; but as a headpiece to English literature, *Beowulf* deserves a most honored position ... it is impossible to deny that the poem has power, a massive strength, and a more than adequate amount of poetic atmosphere. In spite of its digressions, it tells its story well. Best of all, it touches the universal situation of danger to be faced and odds to be overcome, both outward terrors and inward fears.

George K. Anderson, "The Old English Heroic Epic Poems,"
in *The Literature of the Anglo-Saxons.*
Princeton, NJ: Princeton University Press, 1949.

The Unceasing Struggles of *Beowulf's Time*

The barbaric elements in the poem are the strongest and perhaps the most arresting. Life is represented as an endless battle. Man must be ever vigilant against the living forces of evil that attack him from without. At Heorot there is established a great Court where for a time King and retainers dwell in amity and mutual trust. Historical evidence has proved the actual existence of Heorot; but poetically considered, it may be taken as symbolical of human happiness and security persistently assailed by evil powers and threatened with destruction. Beowulf's adventures form but a chapter, so to speak, in the tale of unceasing feud which, with but few intervals, makes up the life of mankind; and his spirit is precisely that of the gods of the old northern mythology, whose last defence lay in the strong right arm and the courageous resolve, and who meet their fate unflinchingly and without surrender.

D.H. Crawford, trans., introduction to Beowulf.
New York: Cooper Square, 1966, p. xii.

Beowulf as a Heroic Sailor

The two [sea] voyages present a direct and simple perfection of action.... The main purpose of these descriptions is to characterize the hero by dramatizing his habitual mode of action. What we are to marvel at, perhaps revel in, when we hear of both voyages is "the achieve of, the mastery of the thing," that sense of easy effortless power and total accomplishment....

In its full implications the image of the hero as sailor is a marvelously effective one, as the authors of the *Odyssey* and *Moby-Dick* knew well. The complex combination of many elements—the skill and prudent discipline of the sailor—warrior, his requisite wary attitude toward the uncontrollable and toward luck, his imperturbable courage, the favoring wind—somehow goes toward creating the image of the hero, who gives himself, commits himself, launches himself boldly (with a sharp weather eye astern) onto a sea that bears him to his destination.

Edward B. Irving, Jr. A Reading of "Beowulf."
New Haven, CT: Yale University Press, 1968.

Grendel's Roots in Scandinavian Folklore

Grendel's nature is, of course, diabolical from a Christian point of view: he is a member of the race of Cain, from whom all misshapen and unnatural beings were spawned, such as ogres and elves. He is a creature dwelling in the outer darkness, a giant, a cannibal. When he crawls off to die, he is said to join the rout of devils in Hell. However, he also appears to have roots in Scandinavian folklore. In Old Norse literature, monsters of his type make their appearance chiefly as *draugar*, or animated corpses. . . . A *draugar* is supernaturally strong and invulnerable (being already dead) and will often have a mother called a *ketta*, or "she-cat," who is even more monstrous than he.

Howell D. Chickering Jr., trans.
introduction to *Beowulf: A Dual-Language Edition*.
Garden City, NY: Anchor Books, 1977.

The Lasting Power of *Beowulf*

Beowulf is one of the relatively few major poems from the distant past which, upon first reading, still capture the attention of the modern reader and leave him changed when he puts the book down. Even those who have felt the narrative method to be flawed have usually responded to the poem's bracing severity, its awesome conflation of dignity and honor, and its strange, autumnal close. To an extent the poem transcends the slow revolutions in literary taste which have taken place since the eighth century: any modern reader can feel its moving power.

Fred C. Robinson, introduction to
*Beowulf: A Verse Translation with Treasures of
the Ancient North*. Berkeley and Los Angeles:
University of California Press, 1983.

Conjuring a Mythic World

The poem possesses a mythic potency. Like Shield Sheafson (as Scyld Scefing is known in this translation), it arrives from somewhere beyond the known bourne of our experience, and having fulfilled its purposes (again like Shield), it passes once more into the beyond. In the intervening time, the poet conjures up a world as remote as Shield's funeral boat borne towards the horizon, as commanding as the horn-pronged gables of King Hrothgar's hall, as solid and dazzling as Beowulf's funeral pyre that is set ablaze at the end. These opening and closing scenes retain a haunting presence in the mind; they are set pieces but they have the life-marking power of certain dreams. They are like the pillars of the gate of horn, through which wise dreams of true art can still be said to pass.

Seamus Heaney, trans., introduction to
Beowulf: A New Verse Translation.
New York: Farrar, Straus & Giroux, 2000.

Chronology

400s A.D.
The Western Roman Empire collapses, and Roman legions and settlers withdraw from the island of Britain.

ca. 460
St. Patrick begins preaching Christianity to the pagan inhabitants of Britain.

ca. 516
At the Battle of Mount Badon, the Celtic Britons defeat the Anglo-Saxon newcomers. The victor of the battle is later said by poets and medieval romancers to be the legendary King Arthur.

ca. 516–525
The Scandinavian king Hygelac undertakes a raid on the coasts of Frisia, during which he is defeated and killed by Frisia's Frankish defenders.

597
Missionaries sent by Pope Gregory and under the leadership of Augustine arrive in Kent in southeastern England. There, they begin the conversion of the Anglo-Saxon kings and settlers to Christianity.

793
The Vikings begin their devastating raids on Britain with the sack of the Lindisfarne monastery, located on an island off the coast of Northumbria.

800s
The poem *Beowulf* is composed by a professional court entertainer and is recorded by a scribe or a literate poet in a form and medium that is now lost.

ca. 1000
The only surviving manuscript of *Beowulf* is created by two different scribes, who copy the poem in the form of prose and bind it into a codex with several other works.

1576
Lawrence Nowell, the dean of England's Litchfield Cathedral, dies; his possessions include the codex that includes *Beowulf.* The earlier whereabouts of the codex are unknown. An Elizabethan antiquarian,

Sir Robert Cotton, acquires Nowell's copy of *Beowulf* and stores it in his extensive library of old books and manuscripts.

1631
Sir Robert Cotton dies and his library is moved to Essex House, an establishment in the London quarter known as the Strand, and then to Little Dean's Yard, a mansion in Westminster.

1731
A fire scorches the *Beowulf* manuscript in Little Dean's Yard.

1753
The *Beowulf* codex is donated to the British Museum, where it remains to this day.

1787
The scholar Grimur Jonsson Thorkelin makes the first two transcriptions of *Beowulf*.

1815
Using his own transcriptions of the poem, Thorkelin produces the first printed version of *Beowulf*. Thorkelin believes *Beowulf* to be a Danish poem that had originally been translated into Old English.

1936
The English scholar and critic J.R.R. Tolkien writes "*Beowulf*: The Monsters and the Critics," derived from his university lecture. Tolkien describes *Beowulf* as a highly accomplished work of art and not just a literary relic of early Christian England. The essay begins the modern era of *Beowulf* studies and interpretation.

Works Consulted

Major Editions of *Beowulf*

Howell D. Chickering Jr., trans., *Beowulf: A Dual-Language Edition.* Garden City, NY: Anchor Books, 1977. A superior translation and reference source that includes a great deal of helpful material in the form of glossaries, notes, and analysis.

D.H. Crawford, trans., *Beowulf.* New York: Cooper Square, 1966. An eloquent and readable verse translation without the line breaks given in other editions in imitation of the poem's original form. This edition includes an introduction, notes, and appendices.

John Earle, *The Deeds of Beowulf: An English Epic of the Eighth Century Done into Modern Prose.* Oxford, UK: Clarendon, 1892. A late nineteenth-century translation of Beowulf; the editor's literary English has itself become dated and has been surpassed by contemporary translations by Seamus Heaney and others.

Seamus Heaney, trans., *Beowulf: A New Verse Translation.* New York: Farrar, Straus & Giroux, 2000. The most popular contemporary translation of *Beowulf.* This version gives the original poem alongside the translator's new version. This translation won glowing reviews and the Whitbread Award, Britain's most prestigious literary prize; while reaching the best-seller lists in 2000 it also brought about a revival of popular interest in *Beowulf.*

Gareth Hinds, *The Collected "Beowulf,"* 2000. thecomic.com. A graphic version of *Beowulf,* collected from three separate volumes, each of which is devoted to a section of the poem. Each volume is created in a different medium: "Grendel" in pen and ink, "The Sea Hag" in woodblock paintings, and "The Dragon" in watercolor.

Ruth P.M. Lehamann, trans., *Beowulf: An Imitative Translation.* Austin: University of Texas Press, 1988. A translation that imitates the meter and alliteration of the original poem. The translator offers background on the poem and a description of her translating methods in the book's introduction.

Frederick Rebsamen, trans., *Beowulf: A Verse Translation.* New York: HarperCollins, 1991. The translator aspires to imitate as clearly as possible Old English verse forms and stress patterns in modern English. The translator breaks into the poem at several points to give background detail and plot summaries, helpful for those struggling with the complex and convoluted story line. The book includes genealogies, a glossary of selected proper names, and a bibliography

Ian Serraillier, *Beowulf the Warrior.* New York: Henry C. Walck, 1961. An abridged prose version of the *Beowulf* story.

Benjamin Thorpe, trans., *Beowulf.* Woodbury, NY: Barron's Educational Series, 1962. A word-for-word transcription and translation of the original Old English text of *Beowulf.*

Donald Tuso, ed., *Beowulf.* New York: W.W. Norton, 1975. The E. Talbot Donaldson prose translation with backgrounds, sources, and criticism.

Literary Criticism of *Beowulf*

Jess B. Bessinger Jr. and Robert F. Yeager, eds., *Approaches to Teaching "Beowulf."* New York: Modern Language Association of America, 1984. A series of essays by literature teachers on the many different ways *Beowulf* can be read and studied in the classroom. The book is divided into sections according to the grade levels and language abilities of the students.

Robert E. Bjork and John D. Niles, eds., *A "Beowulf" Handbook.* Lincoln: University of Nebraska Press, 1997. A book that samples the most important literary debates over *Beowulf.* Each chapter covers a particular topic, giving the background to the debate, the most important contributions to the debate by the various critics and scholars who have taken part, and a summary of further research and analysis to be done. The chapters include "Date Provenance, Author, Audiences," "Diction, Variation, the Formula," "Sources and Analogues," "Digressions and Episodes," and "Christian and Pagan Elements."

Adrien Bonjour, *The Digressions in "Beowulf."* Oxford, UK: Blackwell, 1950. The author describes the stories-within-the-stories that interrupt the main narrative of *Beowulf,* what these digressions signify, and why the poet used them.

Robert B. Burlin and Edward B. Irving Jr., eds., *Old English Studies in Honor of John C. Pope.* Toronto: Toronto University Press, 1974. A collection of scholarly articles on *Beowulf* and other Old English poetry, narratives, and music.

Colin Chase, ed, *The Dating of "Beowulf,"* Toronto, Canada: University of Toronto Press, 1997. A collection of scholarly articles on the dating of *Beowulf,* which present a very wide variety of opinions on the matter. The reader discovers the many historical, literary, and scientific methods applied to the problem of *Beowulf*'s true age.

N.J. Courthope, *A History of English Poetry: The Middle Ages, vol. 2.* London: MacMillan, 1919. This book traces literary ideals inherited from Anglo-Saxon poetry, with the author making the case that the modern English character arises from Anglo-Saxon notions of heroism of the early Middle Ages.

Ursula Dronke, "Beowulf and Ragnarok," *Saga-Book,* Vol. 17, 1969–1970. The author compares and contrasts the Norse legend of Ragnarok and the Christian traditions of the apocalypse in *Beowulf.*

James W. Earl, *Thinking About "Beowulf."* Stanford, CA: Stanford University Press, 1994. An exploration of a variety of aspects of *Beowulf* and other Anglo-Saxon poetry, including the concepts of space and time, history, and early Christianity. The author also discusses the significance of the hall of Heorot and psychoanalyzes the poem using Freudian terms to define the mindset of the poet and his original audience.

Donald K. Fry, ed., *The "Beowulf" Poet: A Collection of Critical Essays.* Englewood Cliffs, NJ: Prentice-Hall, 1968. A series of important essays on *Beowulf,* starting with J.R.R. Tolkien's *"Beowulf:* The Monsters and the Critics" and continuing with literary analysis by Joan Blomfield, Richard Wilbur, Morton Bloomfield, R.M. Lumiansky, Francis Magoun, Rosemary Cramp, Robert P. Creed, Alain Renoir, and Kenneth Rexroth. This book offers a good introduction to the main currents of literary debate over *Beowulf,* although more contemporary critics have been exploring many different aspects of the poem since 1968.

Margaret E. Goldsmith, *The Mode and Meaning of "Beowulf."* London: Athlone, 1970. A book that treats *Beowulf* as a religious and spiritual allegory and explores the poem's action and characters in light of Christian themes such as faith, charity, humility, and salvation. The book gives extensive background on the early Christian church in Britain and on the development of orthodox Christian doctrine during the early Middle Ages. The author extensively quotes and reviews other critics exploring the same themes in contemporary books and essays.

Stanley Greenfield, "The Finn Episode and Its Parallel," *A Critical History of Old English Literature.* New York: New York University Press, 1965. A survey of secular and religious poetry and prose in Old English, with analysis of style, poetic meter, and origins.

Edward B. Irving Jr., *Rereading "Beowulf."* Philadelphia: University of Pennsylvania Press, 1989. This book discusses the aspects of the poem related to its origin as oral poetry and the impact this origin has on the poem's form and language. The author reveals that many difficult and confusing characteristics of *Beowulf* can be traced to its original purpose: the entertainment of a listening audience.

Kevin S. Kiernan, *Beowulf and the "Beowulf" Manuscript.* New Brunswick, NJ: Rutgers University Press, 1981. An exhaustive and expert study of the *Beowulf* manuscript covering the wideranging scholarly debates over the date, provenance, historical context, poetic forms and language of the poem, and offering a meticulous description of the work of the two anonymous scribes who recorded it.

William Witherle Lawrence, *"Beowulf" and Epic Tradition.* New York: Hafner, 1961. The author sets out the literary backgrounds and traditions of *Beowulf*, writing for an audience of casual readers, nonspecialists, and students. The book shows how each of the main episodes and digressions of the poem arose from earlier myths and tales that must have been familiar to the *Beowulf* poet.

Elizabeth M. Liggins, "Revenge and Reward as Recurrent Motives in *Beowulf*." Neuphilologishce Mitteilungen, vol. 74, 1973. The author explores the ancient Germanic traditions of vengeance, and worthy prizes for heroic deeds, and how these customs motivate Beowulf through the course of the epic.

Sarah F. McNary, "Beowulf and Arthur as English Ideals," *Poet Lore*, vol. 6, no. 11, November 1894.

Lewis E. Nicholson, ed., *An Anthology of "Beowulf" Criticism.* Notre Dame, IN: University of Notre Dame Press, 1963. An anthology of eighteen essays covering the literary themes of *Beowulf*, beginning with the turn-of-the-century critic F.A. Blackburn.

Dennis Poupard and Jelena O. Krstovic, eds., *Classical Medieval Literature Criticism, Vol. 1.* Detroit: Gale Research, 1988. An encyclopedic collection of literary criticism on major works of world literature. The *Beowulf* chapter consists of dozens of abridged extracts and is the most useful single collection of commentary on *Beowulf* from early to modern times.

G. Storm, "Grendel the Terrible," Neuphilologische Mitteilungen, vol. 73, 1972. The author analyzes Grendel as a characteristic natural spirit of Germanic poetic tradition.

Joseph Tuso, ed., *Beowulf.* Trans. E. Talbot Donaldson. New York: W.W. Norton, 1975. An anthology of the best-known essays concerning *Beowulf* and its literary merits, along with articles on the background and sources of the poem, joined to E. Talbot Donaldson's prose translation.

William Whallon. "Formulas for Heroes in the *Iliad* and in *Beowulf*" *Modern Philology*, vol. 63, November 1965. The author contrasts the poetic formulas used by the authors in these two epic works, making the point that in *Beowulf*, the formulas are in keeping with the nature of characters, while in the Greek epics these formulas are not always appropriate to the heroes they describe.

Dorothy Whitelock, *The Audience of "Beowulf,"* Oxford, UK: Clarendon, 1951. A collection of three essays on the audience of *Beowulf*, which explore the poem's style and structure by describing the original listeners of the poem and how they responded to it.

Historical Background

Peter Hunter Blair, *An Introduction to Anglo-Saxon England*. Cambridge, UK: Cambridge University Press, 1959. The author draws on archaeological evidence to create a wide-ranging and readable study of Anglo-Saxon England. The book covers Roman Britain, the evidence of place names, the Scandinavian invasions, the Christian conversion, and the unification of England. Separate chapters cover government, the economy, and letters.

David Brown, *Anglo-Saxon England*. Totowa, NJ: Rowman and Littlefield, 1978. A reconstruction of Anglo-Saxon England through archaeological finds, with chapters on the Sutton Hoo ship burial (which many critics have found echoed in the funeral scenes of *Beowulf*), architecture, town design, Viking society in England, and the fate of the Celtic Britons.

G.N. Garmonswey and Jacqueline Simpson, *"Beowulf" and its Analogues*. London: J.M. Dent and Sons, 1968. A useful and fascinating compilation of medieval sources—manuscripts, histories, documents, poetry—related to the *Beowulf* text and broken down by characters in the poem whom the sources describe or identify. This represents an essential book for anyone studying the historical background of *Beowulf*.

Ritchie Girvan, *Beowulf and the Seventh Century: Language and Content*. London: Methuen, 1971. Articles, reports, and criticism for students of *Beowulf*, which also includes new material on the discovery of the Sutton Hoo burial site in England, believed to date from the time of the poem's composition.

John M. Hill, *The Cultural World in "Beowulf."* Toronto, Canada: University of Toronto Press, 1995. A book on the everyday world of *Beowulf*, the traditions of vengeance, kinship bonds, gift giving, and royalty; the concepts of honor and loyalty; and the importance of feuds to the characters of the poem and to the historical Germanic tribes to which they belonged.

Charles N. Kennedy, *The Earliest English Poetry: A Critical Survey of the Poetry Written Before the Norman Conquest with Illustrative Translations*. Oxford, UK: Oxford University Press, 1943. A book about the poetic works contemporary with *Beowulf* and the social milieu from which they arose. The *"Beowulf"* chapter deals with contemporary Scandinavian epics, the historical background of the poem, and the Christian influences on the poet.

Maurice B. McNamee, *Honor and the Epic Hero: A Study of the Shifting Concept of Magnanimity in Philosophy and Epic Poetry*. New York: Holt, Rinehart, and Winston, 1960. A readable description of heroes in epic poetry and how the concepts of honor, duty, and magnanimity to enemies have changed through the years and in different societies.

Sam Newton, *The Origins of "Beowulf" and the Pre-Viking Kingdom of East Anglia*. Cambridge, U.K.: D.S. Brewer, 1994. The author traces the historical royal lineages in *Beowulf* and, while also drawing on archaeology and folklore, makes the case that the poem originated in the turbulent Anglo-Saxon kingdom of East Anglia.

Simon Schama, *A History of Britain: At the Edge of the World? 300 B.C.–A.D. 1603. Vol. 1*. New York: Hyperion, 2000. The first of a two-volume history of Britain covering in its early chapters the prehistory of Britain, the Celtic inhabitants, the Roman invasion, and the Anglo-Saxon invasions that formed the social and cultural background for the *Beowulf* poet.

A.F. Scott, *The Saxon Age: Commentaries of an Era*. Surrey, UK: Croom Helm, 1972. This book contains quotations from contemporary sources on all aspects of Anglo-Saxon England: royalty, town life, families, food and drink, education, the arts, sports, health, work, religion, law, warfare, and trade.

D.M. Wilson, *The Anglo-Saxons*. New York: Frederick A. Praeger, 1962. A richly illustrated archaeological study of the life and customs of early medieval England, including chapters on pagan burials, everyday life, weapons and warfare, and art.

Index

Picture Credits

About the Author

Thomas Streissguth was born in Wasington, D.C., and raised in
Minneapolis. He worked as a teacher, editor, and journalist, and
has traveled widely in Europe, the Middle East, and Southeast
Asia. He has written more than 50 books of nonfiction—
histories, biographies, and geography books—for children and
young adults. He currently lives in Florida.